The Affair of the Lacquered Walnut

by G. H. Teed

First published in the Union Jack magazine,
Series 2, No. 1035, 11 August 1923.

Illustrator unknown

Stillwoods Edition

Stillwoods.Blogspot.Ca

Catalogue Information:
Title: The Affair of the Lacquered Walnut
Author: G. H. Teed (1881-1938)
First published anonymously in the Union Jack magazine, Series 2, No. 1035, 11 August 1923.
Illustrator: unknown
This Edition by: Stillwoods, 2021, (Doug Frizzle)
ISBN Canada: 978-1-989788-54-7
Blog: Stillwoods.Blogspot.Ca
Author Blog: http://ghteed.blogspot.com/
Storefront: http://www.lulu.com/spotlight/lulubook22

Keywords: Sexton Blake, British fictional detective, Tinker, Bryant Kennedy

The library of Teed's stories increases almost daily. Check at the bookstore link above for the latest arrivals. /drf

Cautionary Note: This series of books by Stillwoods are intended to make the stories of G. H. Teed, born in New Brunswick, Canada, available to collectors and researchers. The editor, or rather digitizer has not altered the original publication.

This story may contain language and racial terms that are not appropriate to today. I apologize for them; I know that the author was using his voice to excite and entertain an adventurous English audience. These works were published from 82 to 110 years ago. Most every work has characters of redeeming ethnicity within.

I hope you enjoy and share these stories; I have.
Doug Frizzle

The scene of this grand detective-adventure story is laid in New York and London, ingenious plot, brisk action, and exciting incident are interwoven into a narrative that will be long remembered as one of the most exciting exploits of SEXTON BLAKE and his popular young assistant TINKER.

The U. J. Detective Supplement also appeared in this issue but has not been digitally captured due to image problems —shading and damage issues.

Other Content included a segment from the serial 'The Wire Devils' by Frank L. Packard, another Canadian. This great read which, I believe, is available elsewhere.

The title image shown on the next page shows the reader some of the difficulties in digitizing the contents from this particular issue. I have spent some time cleaning up even this page. Page size indications are about 8 by 11 inches. /drf

The AFFAIR OF THE LACQUERED WALNUT

A TALE OF SEXTON BLAKE AND TINKER

The scene of this grand detective-adventure story is laid in New York and London. Ingenious plot, brisk action, and exciting incident are interwoven into a narrative that will be long remembered as one of the most exciting exploits of SEXTON BLAKE :: and his popular young assistant TINKER. ::

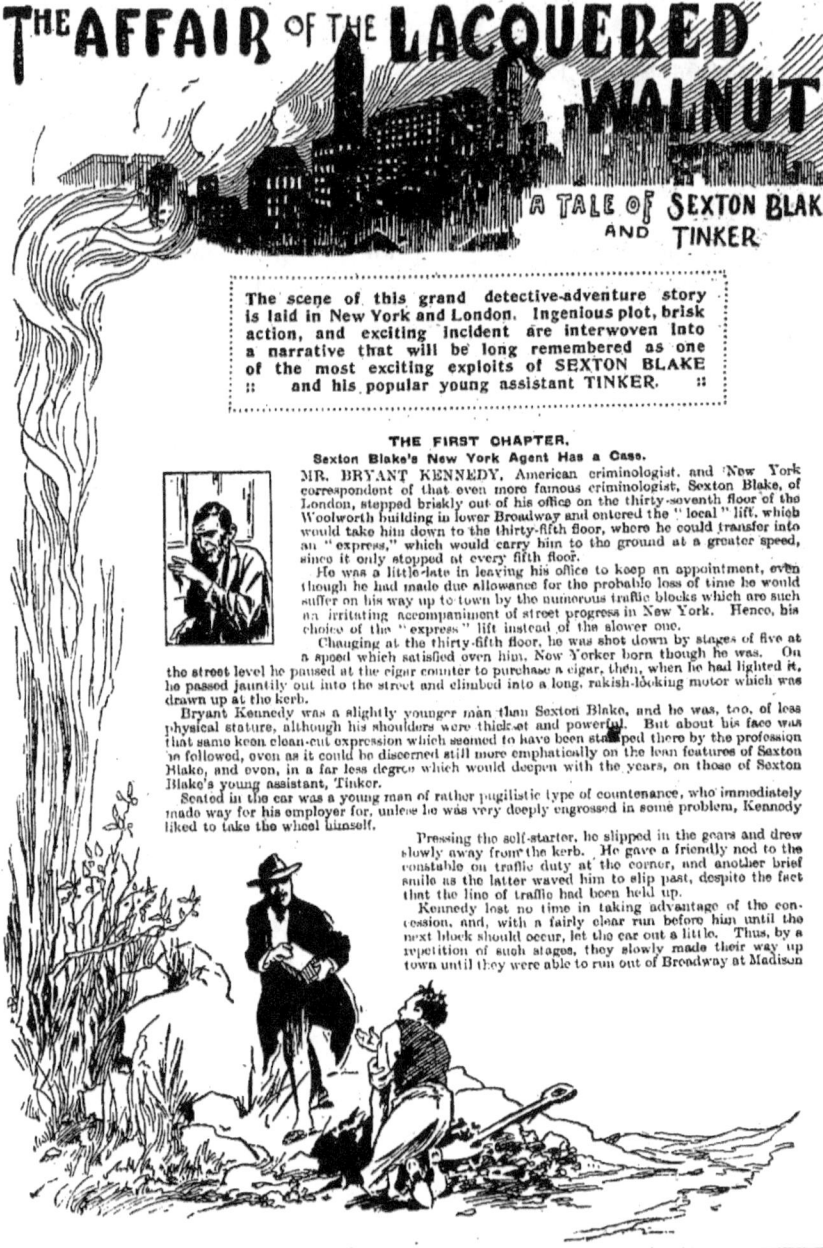

THE FIRST CHAPTER.
Sexton Blake's New York Agent Has a Case.

MR. BRYANT KENNEDY, American criminologist, and New York correspondent of that even more famous criminologist, Sexton Blake, of London, stepped briskly out of his office on the thirty-seventh floor of the Woolworth building in lower Broadway and entered the "local" lift, which would take him down to the thirty-fifth floor, where he could transfer into an "express," which would carry him to the ground at a greater speed, since it only stopped at every fifth floor.

He was a little late in leaving his office to keep an appointment, even though he had made due allowance for the probable loss of time he would suffer on his way up to town by the numerous traffic blocks which are such an irritating accompaniment of street progress in New York. Hence, his choice of the "express" lift instead of the slower one.

Changing at the thirty-fifth floor, he was shot down by stages of five at a speed which satisfied even him. New Yorker born though he was. On the street level he paused at the cigar counter to purchase a cigar, then, when he had lighted it, he passed jauntily out into the street and climbed into a long, rakish-looking motor which was drawn up at the kerb.

Bryant Kennedy was a slightly younger man than Sexton Blake, and he was, too, of less physical stature, although his shoulders were thick-set and powerful. But about his face was that same keen clean-cut expression which seemed to have been stamped there by the profession he followed, even as it could be discerned still more emphatically on the lean features of Sexton Blake, and even, in a far less degree which would deepen with the years, on those of Sexton Blake's young assistant, Tinker.

Seated in the car was a young man of rather pugilistic type of countenance, who immediately made way for his employer for, unless he was very deeply engrossed in some problem, Kennedy liked to take the wheel himself.

Pressing the self-starter, he slipped in the gears and drew slowly away from the kerb. He gave a friendly nod to the constable on traffic duty at the corner, and another brief smile as the latter waved him to slip past, despite the fact that the line of traffic had been held up.

Kennedy lost no time in taking advantage of the concession, and, with a fairly clear run before him until the next block should occur, let the car out a little. Thus, by a repetition of such stages, they slowly made their way up town until they were able to run out of Broadway at Madison

It was at the workman's suggestion that Westmore placed the sapphires in a box and buried them. The location was known only to the two of them. (Chapter 1.)

The First Chapter.   Sexton Blake's New York Agent has a Case.

MR. BRYANT KENNEDY, American criminologist, and New York correspondent of that even more famous criminologist, Sexton Blake of London, stepped briskly out of his office on the thirty-seventh floor of the Woolworth building in lower Broadway and entered the "local" lift, which would take him down to the thirty-fifth floor, where he could transfer into an "express," which would carry him to the ground at a greater speed, since it only stopped at every fifth floor.

He was a little late in leaving his office to keep an appointment, even though he had made due allowance for the probable loss of time he would suffer on his way up town by the numerous traffic blocks which are such an irritating accompaniment of street progress in New York. Hence, his choice of the "express" lift instead of the slower one.

Changing at the thirty-fifth floor, he was shot down by stages of five at a speed which satisfied even him, New Yorker born though he was. On the street level he paused at the cigar counter to purchase a cigar, then, when he had lighted it, he passed jauntily out into the street and climbed into a long, rakish-looking motor which was drawn up at the kerb.

Bryant Kennedy was a slightly younger man than Sexton Blake, and he was, too, of less physical stature, although his shoulders were thickset and powerful. But about his face was that same keen clean-cut expression which seemed to have been stamped there by the profession he followed, even as it could be discerned still more emphatically on the lean features of Sexton Blake, and even, in a far less degree which would deepen with the years, on those of Sexton Blake's young assistant, Tinker.

Seated in the car was a young man of rather pugilistic type of countenance, who immediately made way for his employer for, unless he was very deeply engrossed in some problem, Kennedy liked to take the wheel himself.

Pressing the self-starter, he slipped in the gears and drew slowly away from the kerb. He gave a friendly nod to the constable on traffic duty at the corner, and another brief smile as the latter waved him to slip past, despite the fact that the line of traffic had been held up.

Kennedy lost no time in taking advantage of the concession, and, with a fairly clear run before him until the next block should occur, let the car out a little. Thus, by a repetition of such stages, they slowly made their way up town until they were able to run out of Broadway at Madison Square, and so into Fifth Avenue, where the traffic was equally thick, but where there would be less delay in the wider thoroughfare.

Kennedy continued on up Fifth Avenue until he came to Forty-Seventh Street, where he turned east.

In years gone by, when Delmonico's and Sherry's and Murray's were flourishing, when the Tenderloin district and the "lobster palaces" of the white-light district of New York were in their hey-day, when Jack's was the popular rendezvous for early breakfast by the after-midnight crowd, who knew only too well the merits of Jack's "ham and eggs, Virginia style," and when the popular figures along Broadway were Chauncey Olcott and John Drew, Jim Corbett and Jim Jeffries, Terry McGovern and Kid McCoy, Forty-Seventh Street, like most of the lower forties, was a thoroughfare of some note.

For in it were located several small but very popular hotels and night resorts. But with the passing of the old-time figures, with the demolition of old Rectors, and, through the stress of prohibition, the closing of such resorts as Delmonico's, Murray's, Sherry's, and the Madrid, the resorts along Forty-Seventh suffered equally, and slowly but surely there was a passing away of the old landmarks, until, at the time to which this writing refers, the part into which Bryant Kennedy turned his car that afternoon in early autumn had degenerated into a quarter of third-rate lodging-houses and fourth-rate hotels. It was in very dingy contrast to what it had been ten short years before.

But its appearance mattered not at all to Kennedy, whose profession had made him familiar with quarters east of the Bowery and Houston Street, in comparison to which Forty-Seventh was like a village lane.

He cast a critical eye at some of the more recent changes, noting that they had been none for the better, but drove on steadily until he came to a small private hotel which he had known in his college days as a particularly lively spot after midnight. It was with a faint, reminiscent sigh, as he regarded the shabby exterior of what had once been a bright resort in his own care-free days, that he drew up in front of it. Then, with a word to his man, he descended.

He pushed open the grimy glass door and stalked into the small office, noting that the lounge had been turned into a sort of tea-room, where, he had not the slightest doubt, one could get a drink of bootleg whisky instead of tea if one so desired. The tiny office was still extant, but a sad travesty of its former days, when it had been spotlessly white and bright with bevelled glass. Behind the desk was a frowsy-looking young woman, industriously chewing gum and reading a gaudy journal which purposed to give the heart history of Rudolf Valentino, the then brightest star on the horizon of the movie world.

She essayed a supercilious glance at Kennedy as he approached the desk; but as she took in the cold, hard features and the clothes, which her sharp East Side eyes told her had only come from a downtown tailor or Fifth Avenue, she worked the gum round beneath her tongue and laid Rudolf under the counter for the moment.

It was not often the dingy hotel was entered by men of Bryant Kennedy's type.

For his part, Kennedy knew exactly with whom he had to deal. Hence he anticipated the questions she might have asked. Only a man who knew his New York inside and out could have done it. Without waiting for her to voice her question, he said easily:

"No, I don't wish any tea, nor do I wish a room. I am not even looking for a drink of hootch, and I am not trying to get anything on the house. Now that those preliminaries have been settled, I want to ask you a question, my dear."

The young woman almost swallowed her gum as she jerked her frowsy, blond head.

"Well, sa-ay, can yu beat it?" she murmured in fruity tones. "How do yu get that way, Percy? Whoever whispered to little Gerald that this was a kick joint?"

"Cut that out!" snapped Kennedy. "Come across. You have a lady staying here of the name of Westmorc, I believe. What is the number of her room?"

"So you are looking for the undertaker's candidate in Number Twenty, are you!" she returned. "Well, I'll tell the world that it's about time someone showed up to knock the last tack in the coffin. She's in, Percy, and she'll never go out again, until she's carried out. And, as we're on the subject, perhaps you're the little prodigal with the gold-lined pockets who'll pay what's owin'."

Kennedy threw the girl a glance of contempt, then he snapped his fingers at a cheeky-looking page, who was lounging on a form near at hand, and apparently highly amused at the witticisms of the young woman behind the counter. He grinned cheerfully at Kennedy, but made no attempt to get up. In one stride Kennedy had reached him, and there was a loud wail as the detective jerked him to his feet and planted him on them with a force that shook his teeth.

"The elevator!" snapped Kennedy. And this time, realising that he had to deal with one who knew how to handle the insolence of the "big town," the boy obediently made for the lift. Kennedy followed him in and curtly ordered him to take him to which ever floor Number Twenty was on. This, it appeared, was the first, for the lift stopped there, and Kennedy got out. With a last frown at the boy he strode along until, by reading the numbers above the doors, he came to "twenty." He paused there and tapped on the panels.

There was the sound of movement inside, and a few seconds later the door was opened by a young girl whose rich bronze hair and lovely milky skin fairly took Kennedy's breath away. Her plain black dress was old and well-worn, but the veriest rags could not have dulled that bursting radiant beauty which rose above the black like a flower.

Kennedy bowed, and murmured:

"Miss Westmore?"

"Yes," answered the girl in cool, clear tones. "You are Mr. Kennedy?"

"Yes. I am afraid I am a few minutes late."

"That doesn't matter. Will you come in, please? My mother is ready for you."

Kennedy stepped inside, and, while the girl was closing the door, he made a swift survey of the room. It was a small sitting-room, which still showed signs in its decorations of its former prosperous days, but which now was shabby in the extreme. There was little furniture in the room, and what there was was old and battered. On a couch against one wall a young boy was reclining, and, from what he knew of the persons whom he had come to see, he opined that the lad must be the crippled son of the widow whom he simply knew us Mrs. Westmore.

The lad was a boyish replica of his sister, although his poor little body was shrunken, and twisted with the terrible spinal trouble which had been his heritage. But his eyes were bright and brave, and he smiled cheerfully and frankly at Kennedy as the latter nodded to him.

4

Kennedy walked across and took his hand and, in the way which was such a charming quality of his nature, talked for some time with the boy.

The sister had gone into an adjoining room, but now she returned and nodded to Kennedy. He had a last few cheerful words with the boy, then he followed the girl.

As he passed through the door which she opened he found himself in a small bed-room as dingy as the room he had just left. It was dimly lit, owing to the fact that the single window opened on to a blank wall down which not much daylight could filter.

But there was sufficient illumination for Kennedy to see the form of a woman in the bed in the corner, and as he approached more closely Kennedy saw that her hair, at least, was inherited by the girl. He paused by the bed and took the thin hand which the woman stretched out. Then he sank into the chair that the girl placed for him. The woman in the bed waited until the girl had withdrawn, then she said in low, weak tones:

"It was so good of you to come, Mr. Kennedy. I have been worrying ever since I wrote to you, fearing that perhaps I shouldn't have done so. But I had read of you in the Sunday papers, of several of your cases, and I was so desperate for help that, as a last resort, I risked it."

"If that is the case, then I am sorry you did not write to me before, Mrs. Westmore," answered Kennedy gently. "I should have always been ready to help you if I could. I am sorry to see that you are not well at present, and if you do not feel quite up to telling me why you sent for me, I can arrange to come again when you are feeling better."

"No, no, no!" she cried feverishly. "I —I shall never be better, Mr. Kennedy. I know only too well what illness is mine. It is because of that knowledge I wrote to you, and I shall tell you what is weighing so heavily on my mind, if you will only give me the time and listen."

"I am in no hurry at all, Mrs. Westmore. Take your time, please, and tell me just what your trouble is. If I can help you, rest assured I shall do so."

"When I have done so I shall give you certain papers which will prove what I say. But, first, I will tell you who I am, and how I and my two dear children happen to be in this hideous place.

"I am an Englishwoman, Mr. Kennedy, but my husband was an

American. He was engaged in business in a large way in Germany before the war, but when the war came we tried by every means in our power to get out of the country, While I was suspect, because of my English birth, I was technically an American, and, as in the early days America had not come in, we finally managed to get away.

"In order to do so, however, it was necessary for my husband to make very heavy financial sacrifices. I should, perhaps, have mentioned that his business was dealing in diamonds and other precious stones. He was able to dispose of a good deal of his stock, but just when he was about to transfer the money to the United States, the German authorities, on some technical grounds seized all his funds, or nearly all, for they left him scarcely enough to get us across to England. Luckily he had some consignments of gems at Hatton Garden, and on our arrival in London we realised on those.

Before leaving Germany, warned by his experience, he did not attempt to turn the rest of his stock into money. As it happened, he had disposed of nearly all except a very fine collection of sapphires, which he had hoped to complete in a few months, and dispose of in the form of a unique necklace. But, of course, that was impossible; and, since he was afraid they, too, would be seized if their existence became known, he decided to secrete them until after the war.

"Even that might have been impossible but for the aid of a loyal workman, who had been with him for many years, and who, although he was a German, was faithful to my husband out of gratitude, for some years before my husband had provided the money by which this man was enabled to send his consumptive daughter to a sanatorium, where she was eventually cured.

"It was at his suggestion that my husband placed the sapphires in a box and buried them in a spot of which only he and this workman know the location. At that time, like a good many other persons, we thought the war would not last long; but when it dragged on and on, and finally America came in, my husband joined up. He would have done so before, but for the responsibility of myself and daughter, and, more particularly, of our poor crippled boy.

"He went across to France, and in his first engagement was — was killed."

She broke off then and began sobbing quietly, but Kennedy placed his cool firm hand over her thin ones.

"There are thousands of wives and mothers who have had to

suffer that," he said gently. "Don't dwell on it now, you need your strength for those who are still left to you."

"Alas! It is I who must go next," she whispered. "But I will be calm, Mr. Kennedy, for it is my only hope that you may be able to help me."

She struggled for composure, then she resumed:

"Since my husband left us we have managed to struggle along on what money we had left from the sales of gems he made in London. But that is fast being used up, and, for some time past, I have been trying to plan how I could get possession of the box of sapphires which is buried in Germany. They will not fetch a large fortune, but my husband mentioned that they were worth some fifteen thousand pounds, and if I knew that was safe I could rest easier in the thought that my children would be provided for. It sends me nearly frantic when I think of leaving them penniless, they are so helpless."

"Is this workman of whom you spoke still alive?" asked Kennedy.

"Yes."

"Then it should be easy enough to arrange to get possession of the box of sapphires now that the war is over."

"Ordinarily it would, but certain things make me afraid. I have been in communication with him, and he is ready to smuggle the stones out of Germany as soon as I send him word to do so. It is only some ten months now since I have been in touch with him, but certain things have happened which make me afraid to risk it. I am so helpless lying here, but I can see, and I can draw conclusions."

"I don't quite understand what you mean, Mrs. Westmore. Of what are you afraid?"

"I can't explain exactly. But I have a feeling that someone knows of the existence of the box of sapphires. That they know I am trying to make arrangements to have them smuggled out of Germany. I cannot tell you anything definite to go on, except that I have a constant feeling of being watched, that everything we do and say is known, that our letters are opened and read."

Kennedy's eyes narrowed.

"How long have you been in this hotel?" he asked.

"Nearly a year."

"So you were here when you made your decision to get possession of the box of sapphires?"

"Yes."

"Then it is here, in this hotel, that you have this feeling that you are being spied upon?"

"Yes."

"Um! I think I can promise you that you need have no further fear on that score. It is a pity that, being in ignorance of how this hotel has gone down in the last few years, you came to it, but I shall take good care that things will be made more pleasant for you until you are able to move to more cheerful surroundings. But to return to the subject of our conversation. I take it, you have sent for me to ask me to advise you how to get that box of sapphires out of Germany?"

"Oh, yes, Mr. Kennedy!"

"Then permit me to ask you a few questions.

"You say the box of sapphires is still quite safe where it was buried?"

"Yes. I can show you the letters I have received."

"I shall have those later. And, furthermore, this loyal workman of whom you spoke is prepared to take the risk of smuggling them out of the country?"

"Yes."

"Then it should not be very difficult. If he could get them safely across to London it should be easy enough to arrange the rest. As a matter of fact, I am in close touch with a gentleman in London who is one of the greatest criminologists of the century. You, as an Englishwoman, should know the name —Mr. Sexton Blake."

"Oh! Yes, Mr. Kennedy, I know of Mr. Sexton Blake."

"Very well, Mrs. Westmore. If you will call in your daughter, and ask her to give me the letters of which you have spoken, then I shall work out a plan by which we ought to be able to manage things successfully"

"But these fears which beset me, Mr, Kennedy? I cannot cast aside the feeling that everything I do is known, that there are unscrupulous persons who are scheming to get possession of the box of sapphires as soon as they are brought out of Germany. This place has such an evil atmosphere."

"Don't you worry about that," said Kennedy cheerfully. "You leave that to me, Mrs. Westmore. I know this place all right —have known it for years. I shall take over your affairs, and inside twenty-four hours I shall have a man of my own placed in this hotel who will watch over you and your children. If there is any spying going on we will ditch the spies, never fear. And now I shall call your daughter."

But as Bryant Kennedy settled down a few moments later to read the letters referring to the box of sapphires he was ignorant of two things. The first of those was that no sooner had he ascended in the lift to room No. 20 than the gum-chewing young woman behind the reception desk had pressed a button, which had caused a very shifty-looking young man to appear on the scene.

The second was that, ever since he had been speaking to Mrs. Westmore, each single word of their conversation had been registered by means of a detectorphone, which was placed in the adjoining room, with the receiver in the wall of Mrs. Westmore's bed-room, while the seedy-looking young man was bending over it, an evil smile on his thin, rat-like lips.

The man did not answer, so the taxi-driver touched his arm. At that moment the man fell to one side. As far as the driver could see, he was dead. (*Chapter 2.*)

The Second Chapter. An Appeal from America, and Scotland Yard.

TINKER, the able young assistant to Mr. Sexton Blake, the famous London criminologist, looked up from the cablegram which he had been at work decoding since he and Blake had entered the consulting-room after breakfast, and turned his gaze towards Blake's desk.

"It's from Kennedy, all right, guv'nor, and, as you thought might be the case, it is about that matter on which he wrote."

Blake laid down a letter and swung round in his chair.

"Does it contain anything new, my lad?"

"It certainly does. Shall I read it?"

"Yes."

"He say this, guv'nor:

" 'Reference my letter of the — inst. Most recent report from my agent placed in hotel referred to reveals that in room adjoining that lately occupied by Mrs. W., traces found indicating detectorphone had been in use. Have strong feeling must have been in conjunction with her affairs, and if so confirms her fears that she was being spied upon. Discovery inclines me belief that forces are at work to secure box referred to my letter. Advise caution. Leave everything your discretion, but feel sure attempt will be made. Am writing full particulars. Advise me sharp if you would like me come to London.— KENNEDY.' "

Blake tapped his teeth with the end of a pencil, then he reached absent-mindedly for the big silver box of cigarettes, selected one, and lit it.

"So Kennedy has uncovered traces of spying in that hotel in Forty-Seventh Street?" he remarked thoughtfully. "Um! Rather pity he did not light on it before. If Mrs. Westmore —that is the lady's name, I believe, isn't it —was being watched by some crooks, who, in some way, had got to know about the box of sapphires of which Kennedy wrote us, then it wouldn't be unlikely that they also knew she had sought Kennedy's assistance."

"It seems to me, guv'nor, with all due respect to Mr. Kennedy, that if, as he says, Mrs. Westmore was being spied on at that hotel, then the spies must have known pretty well what it was Kennedy was planning to do. What I mean is, it is on the cards that they already know you are mixed up in it."

"That is certainly a possibility, my lad. Of course, we do not know the exact conditions of Kennedy's interview, or interviews, with Mrs. Westmore. I can't recollect that he mentioned those details in his letter."

"No, sir, he did not. He just stated the facts of how he had been sent for by that lady, and had called on her at a hotel in Forty-Seventh Street, mentioning that it was a hotel which had got down at heels of recent years. He added, if you will remember, that he had arranged for the lady and her two children to be taken to his mother's house in Washington Square."

"Ah, yes! I recall that now, my lad. By the way, it is about four days, isn't it, since we received his letter?"

"Five days to-day, guv'nor."

"Why, then our man should have arrived at the Venetia last night, or, at the very latest, he should arrive to-day, if he follows the instructions which Kennedy says he gave him by the same mail that brought his letter to us, and of course, if the man in Germany succeeded in getting past the frontier with the box of sapphires. Did you telephone to the Venetia last night?"

"I telephoned yesterday afternoon, as well as the night before last, and I telephoned last evening about eleven —just before you got back from that banquet."

"Browning had heard nothing?"

Browning was the manager of the Venetia Hotel.

"Not a word, sir; and if our man had turned up he would have tried to get in touch with you at once —that is if he followed Mr. Kennedy's instructions."

"And now Kennedy cables that the man he placed on duty in the hotel in Forty-Seventh Street has discovered traces that a dictaphone had been installed in the room next to that occupied by Mrs. Westmore, and warns us to be on our guard. H'm! Well, now, according to your figures, the man we expect from Germany is twenty-four hours or more late.

"It may well be that he has found some difficulty in getting across into Holland or Belgium with his contraband, and that is the reason of his delay.

"On the other hand, in view of the contents of this cable, we mustn't overlook the possibility that Kennedy's plans were known, and that we have been forestalled. If he has definite suspicions of anyone, why hasn't he made inquiries more fully? If there were spies planted at that hotel, then he should be able to get some sort of a description of them.

"It ought not to be very difficult, to get a line on the person, or persons, who occupied that room just before he went to see Mrs. Westmore."

"Well, he doesn't say a word about that, guv'nor."

"No. Well, all we can do, for to-day at least, is to sit tight and see if our man turns up by to-night. Even if he doesn't, I don't see what we can do. We have no moans of knowing whether he has started from Germany or no, and, of course, there is always the possibility that he may 'double-cross' us, despite what Kennedy says about his faithfulness to the Westmores. We mustn't forget that, after all, he is a Boche."

"There is the street bell, guv'nor. Shall I go? Mrs. Bardell is busy downstairs."

"Yes, see who it is."

Tinker rose, and Blake turned back to his work, but he swung round in his chair again as the lad ushered in Inspector Thomas, of Scotland Yard. Blake shook hands with the inspector, and motioned to the saddlebag chair close to the desk; then he pushed across a box of cigars, from which the inspector carefully selected and lit one. When he had it going to his satisfaction he leant back in the chair, and said:

"I'm a little early this morning, Blake, but I want you to come along to the Yard, and see if you can identify the body of a man there. He was found strangled in a taxi last night, and the only clues we have been able to discover, so far, are two slips of paper, on one of which is your name and address."

Blake's eyes narrowed in perplexity.

"A man found strangled last night, and on him you find a slip of paper bearing my name and address? I don't understand, inspector. But you said there were two slips. What was on the second?"

"The name of the Hotel Venetia."

"And that is all?"

"Everything. But I have brought the taxi-driver along with me. Shall I have him in and let him tell his story?"

"By all means. Let Tinker call him."

Blake said nothing, while the lad departed to summon the man who was seated in the cab which had brought the inspector to Baker Street. He lit a fresh cigarette, and as the man entered he shot a keen glance at him, then he waited for Inspector Thomas to give his instructions. At a word from the man from Scotland Yard, the taxi-driver— a stoutish, respectable-looking man, whose appearance was typical of his calling— shuffled forward, fingering his cap a little nervously as he faced the famous detective. But he told his story in a perfectly straightforward manner.

"It's like this here, sir," he said. "I was driving slowly along the Strand last evening, looking for a fare, when I was hailed by a man standing on the kerb."

"What time was this?" asked Blake curtly.

"Between nine and a quarter past, sir."

"What was the appearance of the man who hailed you?"

"He was a big bloke, sir —about six feet or more, I should say, and very thick in the build."

"His age, approximately —his clothing —was he clean-shaven, or not? Give me all the points you can."

"He was well enough dressed, sir, but I should say, from his hat and his accent, that he was either an American or a Colonial. Anyway, he was no Englishman, although I won't say he wasn't Irish. He had a moustache, and, I fancy, he was about forty or thereabouts. But you understand, sir, I didn't size him up very closely."

"Very well. Go on with your story."

"Well, sir, he wanted for to go to the East India Docks. I wasn't very keen on the journey at that hour of the night, as I know it wouldn't be easy to get a return fare, but he said he was coming straight back, and, as he offered me ten bob over and above the clock, I took him aboard.

"I drove him through to the docks, and pulled up outside the upper gates while he went inside. He wasn't gone more'n a quarter of an hour or so before he comes out again in tow with a little man. They got in, and the big 'un told me to drive to the Hotel Venetia. I came back up west, and, according to my instructions, pulled in at the kerb in front of the Venetia, or, shall I say, just a couple of cab's lengths before I got to the hotel, which, you will know, sir, is just in front of a shop which is closed at that hour of the night."

"Why did you pull in there, instead of driving right up to the entrance?"

"Because one of them tapped on the window."

"I see. What next?"

"Well, sir, the big 'un gets out, and stands at the door of the cab talking to the other for a few minutes. I hears him say he won't be more than ten minutes at the outside, and then he tells me to pull on to the rank, and wait there. He closed the door and went into the hotel. I then drove on to the rank in the middle of the road.

"I had a pipe and a few words with one of my mates who was on the rank, and I was with him until he was signalled for from the hotel. That was a matter of fifteen minutes or so. Thinks I to myself, it's about time my fare was showing up, so I stood by the bonnet of my cab with an eye on the hotel entrance. Maybe another ten minutes or so went by, and then another of my mates drove on to the rank. I walked along to have a word with him, and maybe another ten minutes went by— call it half an hour, all in all sir.

"Then I comes back to my cab, and takes a glance inside to see if the other gent is getting impatient. As I did so, I noticed he was slumped down in one corner in a funny way, sir.

"I thought, maybe, he had gone to sleep, but, just to make sure, I opened the door and climbed in and spoke to him. He didn't answer, so I touched his arm. At that he just fell over on one side, and I smelt something wrong.

"As far as I could figure, sir, he was as dead as Charlie Peace, so I closes the door and reports the matter to the nearest constable on duty. He makes an examination, and then orders me to drive on to Scotland Yard, which I did. That is all I know about the affair, sir."

"And what became of your other fare?"

"That I can't tell you, sir."

"It was a plant," put in Inspector Thomas. "As soon as this man brought his cab to the Yard, I took charge of matters. I got on the telephone at once to the Venetia, and gave a description of the other man to Browning, the manager. He had inquiries made, and, about half an hour later, phoned me that the commissionaire on duty at the Regent Street entrance had noticed a man answering to that description pass out during the evening.

"By close questioning, the time was set at just about that which this man declared was the time he reached the Venetia —about twenty minutes to eleven. If the man who entered the hotel at that hour, and the man who passed out at the Regent Street entrance are one and the same, then it looks as if he walked straight through the hotel and made his getaway."

"It looks that way, I must confess. But, you say the man found in the cab had been strangled?"

"That is so. The doctor was positive on that point. Of course, there will be a post-mortem."

"But when was he strangled? The driver says the other was carrying on a conversation with the man after he had emerged from the cab. He couldn't have strangled his companion while he was standing on the pavement."

"That is exactly why I have come on to see you. I can't figure it out at all."

Blake turned to the driver.

"You are quite positive that the two conversed before the big man closed the door?"

"Dead certain, sir. Why, I recollect part of their conversation. The big 'un said something about making someone in the hotel pay the account before he left, or he would take legal proceedings, and the man inside said something in agreement."

"Um! Distinctly curious. You drove straight on to the rank?"

"Yes, sir."

"And were close to your cab all the time?"

"I wasn't ten feet away at any one time, and then the cab was in full view. It couldn't have been done then."

"In that case, it must have been done before the big man got out of the cab. And yet, men who are strangled to death don't afterwards carry on a conversation with the human voice. Had the job been done by the hands, inspector?"

"Yes. There was no cord or anything of that sort. Only a very powerful man could have done it in such a way as not to attract the attention of the driver; and the man we want fits that qualification."

"In that case, one thing is obvious."

"What is that, Blake?"

"The driver is mistaken. He did not hear the man inside the cab speak."

"But I tell you, sir, I heard him as plain as could be."

"You did not, my man. You may honestly think you did, but, if that man was already dead, you certainly did not hear him speak."

"I ain't no believer in ghosts, sir."

"You don't need to be to explain the puzzle. You thought you heard the man inside speak. What you really heard was a faked conversation, carried on by one man alone; the big man, by his ruse, was able to get a half-hour's clear start for his get-away."

"B-but, sir, how could that be?"

"I don't follow, either, Blake," put in the inspector.

"It is not difficult," answered Blake. "One word will explain it."

"What is that?"

"Ventriloquism," said Blake succinctly.

DETECTORPHONE

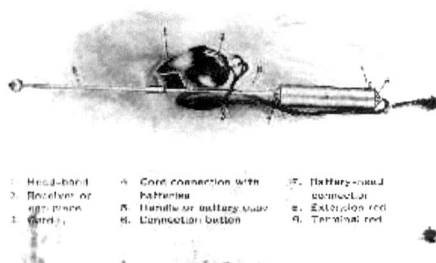

1. Head-band
2. Receiver or ear-piece
3. Cords
4. Cord connection with batteries
5. Handle or battery case
6. Connection button
7. Battery-head connector
8. Extension rod
9. Terminal rod

DIRECTIONS

1. See that all joints are screwed tightly into place.

2. Hold the apparatus so that the disc on the end of terminal rod 9 is at right angles with the ground, or nearly so. If either of the flat sides of the disc faces the ground the Detectorphone is inoperative.

3. Press the point of the disc against the part to be tested for sound. Put on the head-band, place the ear-piece to the ear and press the button. In listening for a faint sound, or when working near noisy machinery or other disturbing sounds, stop up one ear with the finger and place the ear-piece to the other.

4. If the Detectorphone sounds "dead," ascertain if the button. No. 6, is firmly pressed down.

5. The terminal rod, No. 9, may be used without the extention rod, No. 8, if the latter is not needed to increase the length.

6. When putting in a fresh battery, notice the brass plug in the end of the battery. Insert the battery into the handle or battery case, No. 5, so that this brass plug is in contact with battery-head connection, No. 7.

7. A little experience in testing the sounds made by your engine, bearings, other parts of machinery, water pipes, etc, when in good order, will enable you to detect the slightest defect. All defects, whether broken balls, sand or dirt in bearings, or more obscure defects in machinery, create noises of their own which can be quickly detected and located before damage is done. Noise means loss of power and waste of money

M'f'g'd by The DETECTORPHONE Dept. B. T. M. Co.

41 West Street, Boston, Mass.

Detectorphone   /drf

"BY heavens; I never thought of that!" exclaimed Inspector Thomas.

"I can see no other way to explain it," went on Blake. "The man was dead when he was found in the cab. The doctor at the Yard stated the cause of death to be strangulation. Unless the man strangled himself, which is quite impossible with just the hands, then he must have been dead before his companion got out at the Venetia.

"Therefore, the conversation, or rather, the supposed conversation, which the driver heard, was, in reality, a monologue in which the murderer used ventriloquial powers to fool the driver. A neat idea if a man is gifted in that way, and by no means rare in the annals of crime. But, even if that theory should prove to be the correct one, I am still extremely puzzled about the two slips of paper which you found on the victim."

"Can't you place the man?"

"I might, or might not, recognise him when I have seen the body. Otherwise it would be risky to commit myself. Besides, you have given me no detailed description of him. All I know is what the driver has told me."

"The description is easy. He is, or was, a smallish man, a trifle over fifty, I should say. He was not English; he is of German appearance, and his overcoat bears the label of a Berlin clothing firm."

Blake shot a glance at Tinker, but made no comment on the inspector's last statement.

"Perhaps it would be best for me to have a look at the body, as you suggest. Are you sure nothing else was found on him?"

"Nothing; no papers, or anything to reveal his identity. But I have discovered that he arrived yesterday afternoon at the docks in a small cross-Channel packet from Antwerp, so it looks as if he must have come through from either Belgium or Germany."

"Is the cab you came in the one in which he was killed?"

"Yes."

"Nothing found in it?"

"No —or, rather, we did find something, but apparently it has no connection with the affair."

"Ah! What was found, inspector?"

The inspector did not answer at once, but, thrusting his hand in his pocket, drew out a smallish round object, which he passed across to Blake.

Taking it between his thumb and first finger, Blake held it up, and it could be seen that it was simply an ordinary walnut, rather smaller than one usually finds on the market. That is the impression it gave one; but after his first glance Blake bent over it with a sudden interest, for he had noticed that the walnut had been very neatly lacquered over the whole surface.

For some minutes he turned it over and over in his hand. Then:

"Did you notice that this walnut had been lacquered, inspector?"

"I noticed it had been treated in some way. Someone had a lot of time to spare, I fancy."

"Do you mean to say you don't know what use this walnut was put to —or, at least, the use for which it was intended?"

"Why, what else but to be eaten?" ejaculated the inspector a little impatiently.

"Wrong, my dear fellow," drawled Blake. "And I believe you have been in China, too."

"Well, what of that? What has that walnut got to do with China? And what can it have to do with the murder in the taxi?"

"Not so fast—not so fast! To begin with, the lacquering is certainly either the work of a Chinaman or a Japanese —Eastern, at any rate. Now, if you had taken the trouble to investigate a few of the ordinary customs of China, inspector, you would have found that among certain classes of Chinese —more particularly the mandarin and scholarly classes —it is considered a great aid to the calm mental examination of a subject to roll a couple of lacquered walnuts together in the hand.

"It is a most fascinating occupation to watch. Round and round they go as the hand moves automatically, and a keen observer can at times pretty well guess at what pace the mind of the thinker is working by watching the speed at which he rolls the walnuts.

"It is said, too, that it is an indication of the state of the thinker's temper. At any rate, the nearest the average Celestial ever comes to exhibiting his feelings is the rate of speed at which he rolls the walnuts. Did you not know that?"

"I did not. Are you serious?"

"Perfectly. It is easy enough for you to examine the subject in detail. Every man almost who knows anything at all about China knows of the custom."

"Well, I never heard of it. And, anyway, what has that walnut to do with the murder?"

"That I cannot say. But we might extend our theory a little if we could discover just how the walnut happened to get in the cab. In the first place, the driver may have had an Oriental passenger who was addicted to the habit and who inadvertently dropped one of his walnuts. Or, again, he may have had a fare who had acquired the habit in the East and practised it wherever he might be. And a third possibility is that it may have been dropped by one of the pair he last drove yesterday evening. You did not find another walnut on the person of the victim?"

"No."

"Well, perhaps the driver can enlighten us."

"I didn't drive no Chinkies, sir," announced the driver. "Nor I didn't have no other fare last evening until I picked up the big 'un in the Strand. I was at home for my supper at six o'clock, and if that there walnut had been in the cab my nipper would have found it when he cleaned out the cab. That is his job, and he does it regular before I go out."

"Ah! He cleaned it as usual last evening?"

"That he did, sir, and washed it as well."

"That process would include taking out the mat from the bottom and beating it, I suppose?"

"Yes, sir."

"Then you are inclined to think the walnut would not be in the taxi when you left your house last evening?"

"That's it, sir."

"You think, then, it must have been dropped by one of the two men you drove to the Venetia?"

"I do, sir."

Blake turned back to the inspector. "If that should prove to be the case, then it is quite possible that this walnut may be a not unimportant clue. If it should have been dropped by the murderer — why, it is doubly important. We have a fair description to go on already. If he is a professional crook, then that habit of rolling a couple of walnuts— if he possessed the habit —must have marked him in some circles at least. I should say it was worth following up, inspector."

The inspector grunted, as if incredulous, but inwardly he was digesting every word Blake uttered. Inside a few minutes he had heard the famous detective build up a theory around what he had considered to be a quite unimportant trifle, which, if it could be proved to be so, would be a most important clue.

But at the moment he was keen on getting Blake to view the body of the murdered man, for he had not entirely missed Blake's swift glance in Tinker's direction when he had stated that the man had probably arrived in London from either Belgium or Germany, and the inspector was highly intrigued to know why a man of that sort should have nothing on his person except two slips of paper, one of which bore the name of the Baker Street criminologist, and the other the name of a hotel which was frequented more by Blake than any other hotel in London.

The inspector was a little slow on the uptake, but he had not reached the position he held at the Yard without possessing a very well balanced mentality, and he had figured that his best move was to find out just what association, if any, Blake might have with the unknown victim of an equally unknown assassin. Nor was he forgetting that if Blake's suggestions could be proved to be based on fact, then he had another very important clue in the suggestion that ventriloquism had been used by the assassin in order to deceive the taxi-driver.

"I'll follow that up," he said finally, "when you have seen the body. Why not come along now? It will have to be shifted soon."

"I don't mind. Shall we go along in the cab?"

"If you wish."

"Very well. Tinker and I will both come. By the way, have you the slips of paper with you?"

"No; they are at the Yard. I will show them to you when we get there."

"All right. Get your cap, Tinker, and bring along my hat with you."

Tinker went off to obey, and in a few minutes was back again. Then Blake rose, and all four passed out to the street, where the cab stood. The driver took his place at the wheel, while Blake, the inspector, and Tinker, got inside.

On the way to Scotland Yard, Blake made a superficial examination of the interior of the cab, but without coming upon anything that suggested any fresh line of thought. If the lacquered walnut was all it had yielded, or would yield, then he realised it was, after all, very little to go on.

At the same time Blake knew the walnut was undoubtedly one that had been prepared specially for the odd Chinese custom which he had described to the inspector, and, while he would have thought little of such a discovery in, say, a rickshaw in Canton or Shanghai, he was forced to view it from an entirely different angle when the discovery had been made in a London taxicab.

As Inspector Thomas had informed them, the body of the murdered man had been taken to the Yard the previous evening, and it was still lying in a small room there. On their arrival, the inspector led them immediately to the room in question, and both Blake and Tinker made a close examination of the unknown victim.

But when they had emerged from the room, and in answer to the inspector, had informed him that they had never set eyes on the man before they told only the truth.

But Blake did not add what both he and Tinker were thinking — that they suspected there was a very big chance that the victim was none other than the man of whom Bryant Kennedy had written them, and who, if he succeeded in getting out of Germany with the box of sapphires belonging to Mrs. Westmore, was to make for the Hotel Venetia, in London, and from there communicate with Sexton Blake.

In the inspector's private room at the Yard this suspicion was strengthened in the mind of both Blake and the lad, for no sooner had their eyes fallen on the two slips of paper which the inspector produced than they at once recognised Kennedy's handwriting.

Kennedy had written to Blake that he had given written instruction to the man in Germany, and here, with the name of the Venetia, and Blake's name and address written in the New Yorker's own fist, and found on the person of one whose clothing bore the label of a Berlin firm, it certainly looked like conclusive proof.

But what both Blake and Tinker were wondering at that moment was —what had become of the box of sapphires?

Were they the motive of the crime? And were they now in the possession of the man who, in addition to being no mean ventriloquist, appeared to possess at least one common custom peculiar to the Yellow Empire of the East?

At the present stage of affairs Blake was not inclined to take the inspector completely into his confidence. At the same time he realised that it was his duty to give the Yard official any hint possible which might assist him in the casting of the police net; for if the box of sapphires had been secured by the man who had strangled Kennedy's agent —always presuming that the victim had been the agent in question, then it was a safe bet that he would lose no time making his get-away from England.

And the man who could so coolly walk off in a busy thoroughfare like Piccadilly, leaving his victim dead in a public taxi, would be able to bring into play other ruses quite as difficult to combat.

Therefore, Blake made a statement to the inspector, which gave that official as much suggestion of value as if Blake had told him all that Kennedy had written.

"As I have said, I have never seen this man before," he remarked, when he handed back the two slips of paper. "On the other hand, I recognise the handwriting on these bits of paper. But that handwriting is not of the man who lies dead in the room beneath, nor is it of the murderer. It is the hand of a man in New York, whose identity I am not at liberty to give you at present.

"I suspect that the murdered man came to England to see me. I was expecting a man from Germany on a private matter and I am inclined to think the man found in the cab was he."

"Then you know the motive for the crime?"

"I think so. All I am prepared to say now is that, in my opinion, the motive was robbery. By what person, or persons, I cannot guess, but I will venture the tentative theory that the taxi-driver was right — that is that the big man who gave him the slip at the Venetia was either an American, or one who had lived in that country long enough to get the accent, because I believe his crime was conceived in New York.

"He may or may not have been playing a lone hand. I don't know. But I shall get what information I can without delay, and pass it on to you. In the meantime, I would suggest that you send out a description of the man in question to all stations, and I would make a prominent note of the fact that he is a ventriloquist of some attainment, and also is addicted to the Chinese habit of rolling two lacquered walnuts in one hand.

"I would lay particular stress on the latter, because, even if he is too cautious to indulge in the habit openly since losing one walnut last night, he will find it quite impossible to refrain from mechanically moving his hand in that manner when he is not on guard.

"And one last word, inspector, if my theory of the motive is correct, then he must have got away with loot of considerable value, for I suspect it consisted of a box of precious stones —sapphires, to be exact. That is all I am in a position to say just now."

"Well, if you are right, you have given us something to go on, and I shall certainly get the net out at once. Will you take a hand with us?"

"You must count me out for the present. As I said, I am simply making statements on a theory based on certain things which have come to my knowledge. But rest assured, inspector, as soon as I am in a position to do so, I shall pass on any further information which comes to my knowledge."

And knowing how useless it would be to press Blake, the inspector refrained from doing so. Before they left, Blake got from the inspector the name of the cross-Channel packet by which the murdered man had reached London, and as soon as he and Tinker were in Whitehall, he said:

"You go on to the docks, my lad, and find this packet, if she has not left again. Find out what you can about the man who was strangled. In the mean time, I shall go on to Baker Street, and get off a cablegram to Kennedy. I cannot help but think that his agent at the hotel in Forty-Seventh Street was stupid not to have discovered sooner about the detectorphone connection. Had he done so, and had Kennedy cabled us sooner, we might have prevented what occurred last night."

"I think so, too, guv'nor. It certainly looks as if the man who was killed was heading for Baker Street all right"

"There is not the slightest doubt in my mind. But we are not in a position to make such a definite statement to the inspector. Now, off with you!"

As soon as Tinker had departed for the docks in one taxi, Blake hailed another, and drove back to Baker Street. When he was again seated at his desk he lit a cigarette, and, leaning back in his chair, gave himself up to thought.

He did not stir until the ash of the cigarette was almost burning his lips, then he sat up with a jerk, tossed the end of the cigarette away, and took down his private volume of Bentley's code. With this before him, he began to make up a cable to Bryant Kennedy; and it was evident that it was a message of some length, for he was more than half an hour engaged on the job.

When he had finished, the sheet of paper was practically covered with several lines of apparently meaningless ten-letter words; but when Bryant Kennedy should receive it, and decode it, he would find that Blake had cabled him as follows:

"Unknown man was found strangled last evening in taxicab. Crime evidently committed between river docks in East End and Hotel Venetia. Only items found on body two slips of paper bearing name Venetia, my name and address, respectively; both slips in your handwriting. Label of clothing bears name Berlin shop. Inclined think victim your messenger who was coming through on matter mentioned your letter. Cable, sharp, full description if possible secure. No sign whatever of box mentioned your letter; appears murderer must have secured. Scotland Yard working and have certain clues to go on. Inquire and telegraph sharp if anything known of your side criminal following description and characteristics. At least six feet, heavy, powerful build, about forty years age, considerable ability as ventriloquist, and probably has Chinese habit rolling two lacquered walnuts in one hand. Suggest you make further inquiries hotel Forty-Seventh Street. Will follow up any clues this end. Urgent.—BLAKE."

"I fancy that covers the essentials," he muttered, as he wrote the word "URGENT" in heavy ink at the top and lifted the receiver to phone for a messenger.

"If that murder did have its inception at New York, then it is a pretty good bet that the person, or persons, who set up that detectorphone in the hotel in Forty-Seventh Street got the dope that way. In that case, Kennedy ought to be able to dig up something. At any rate, I have given him a line to go on. What he should have done, instead of trusting to a letter, was to come across himself. He ought to sack that stupid ass who only found traces of the detectorphone days after it had fulfilled its purpose. Had he done so, and had Kennedy acted sharp, the whole thing might have been prevented."

Blake was still smoking and ruminating when Tinker returned from his visit to the docks. As soon as he entered Blake glanced at him inquiringly.

"Well?" he asked curtly.'

"I found the tub all right, guv'nor— some tub, too, believe me. I got hold of the captain. He didn't speak much English, but with my French we managed to get along. He couldn't tell me much about the man whose description I gave him, although he recognised that quick enough.

"He told me, what practically confirms the taximan's story —that a big man appeared last evening and asked for the man in question. It appears he was on the passenger-list as one Carl Schonberg, and I proved that, because I went into his cabin and searched through his bag. I found a few items of clothing, and a German passport, which had been vised for Belgium and England. I can't figure out how he managed to get ashore last night without it,"

"Nor can I. Some hanky-panky there, my lad. But, go on. Anything else?"

"That, is about all, guv'nor. I pinched the passport, and brought it along for you to see. The captain didn't know anything at all about the man —simply said he had come aboard at Antwerp, and that, his passport being in order, he had allowed him to come across."

"Um! Well, toss the passport on the desk, Tinker. I will examine it after lunch. I have coded an urgent cable lo Kennedy, and have phoned for a messenger. As soon as he turns up, get it away. I am going into the laboratory for half an hour. Call me as soon as lunch is served."

With that Blake stalked off and remained in the laboratory until Tinker went along to call him for lunch. The cable had been sent almost immediately after Blake's departure from the consulting-room, and since it had been sent, "urgent" (at triple rate), a reply should be received during the afternoon.

As a matter of fact, Blake and Tinker had finished the biggest part of the afternoon's work, and were idling over tea, when the answer came. Tinker jumped at once to decode it, and, as soon as he had finished he passed it across to Blake.

This is what Kennedy had to say:

"'Reference your telegram description agent referred to in letter as follows (then there came a detailed description which was sufficient to convince Blake beyond the shadow of a doubt that the man who lay dead at Scotland Yard could be none other than the man who had tried to get through from Germany with the box of sapphires). Your news great shock, and am preparing leave at once for

England. Reference your inquiry regarding criminal possessing characteristics named, have ascertained well-known crook known as Shanghai Charlie was liberated Sing Sing three months ago. Is clever ventriloquist, and stool pigeon here informs me Shanghai Charlie lived some years in China, and had acquired habit rolling two walnuts. Further inquiries my agents reveal only to-day crook known as Rat the Finn was living some weeks at hotel in Forty-Seventh Street during residence there my client occupied adjoining room. Undoubtedly Rat the Finn who rigged the detectorphone. Before Shanghai Charlie was sent Sing Sing last stretch he and Rat the Finn worked together. Make note Shanghai Charlie said to be a strangler, who never uses knife or gun. Description Rat the Finn as follows: Very small shrunken frame, clean-shaven, weasel features, slightly stooped, believed consumptive, voice high-pitched whining, eyes close set watery blue, nose long very thin pointed, invariably wears bowler hat or cap, inveterate cigarette smoker, and has habit talking cigarette in mouth, wanted here on several charges, two being murder. Is said to use both knife and gun, and very fine shot. Suspect he and Shanghai Charlie behind crime mentioned. Please use every effort apprehend. Will cable what steamer arriving by.—KENNEDY.'"

Blake laid the paper down.

"What do you make of that, my lad?"

"It strikes me if Mr. Kennedy's man had discovered some of those facts before, we could have spoilt that game last night," replied Tinker briefly;

"You have said it, my lad. As it is, it looks as if two choice criminals, one known as Shanghai Charlie and the other as Rat the Finn, were loose on this side of the Atlantic. One of the gentlemen appears to specialise in strangling, the other to be expert with both knife and gun. That seems to point to Shanghai Charlie as the one who killed the poor devil, who, despite his nationality, seems to have been quite faithful to his trust. It is indeed, as you say, my lad, distinctly a pity we did not know all this before."

"What will you do, guv'nor?"

"Do? Why, my lad, do you think we are going to let that pair of rats get away with this murder and the box of sapphires as well?"

Tinker grinned.

"I didn't imagine you would," he said.

"You are quite right. You pull a chair up here and I will tell you the first steps we shall take."

Tinker's eyes reverted to the dangling right hand of the big man, and, even as the other made his run and released the ball, Tinker saw the fingers close and mechanically work round and round against the palm—just as he had seen a Chinaman perform the action when rolling a couple of lacquered walnuts.
(Chapter 4.)

IN considering the plan which he had determined he and Tinker should follow, Blake, naturally, took into full consideration the fact that Scotland Yard would have its net out, and that there was a very big chance that the Yard would succeed in catching the man he and Tinker now suspected of being Shanghai Charlie before the strangler could escape from the country.

In view of the additional strength given to Blake's suspicions, he thought it his duty to communicate the principal contents of Kennedy's cablegram to Inspector Thomas, and this he did that same day before he and Tinker left the house.

Nevertheless, consideration of what the Yard might or might not do did not affect Blake's plans in the slightest.

Should either he or Tinker succeed in running down the strangler, it would, of course, be their duty to hand him over to the police.

But what Blake was even more keen on running to earth was the box of sapphires, which had completely disappeared, following the murder of the man they had good reason to believe was the German who had smuggled them through from Germany on behalf of Mrs. Westmore, Kennedy's client.

While Blake felt that Kennedy's man in New York had bungled the case at that end, he would not relax his efforts to do all in his power to assist his New York correspondent, for, in the past, Bryant Kennedy had been of no little value to him in several American cases.

Therefore, he went ahead just as if the Yard knew nothing at all about the matter. Blake realised that if the man they sought was Shanghai Charlie, there was every possibility that he had not yet managed to get out of London. It was more than likely that he would lie low somewhere until he found out just what police suspicions or activities were to follow the coup he had pulled off at the Venetia.

This being so, then their biggest chance of locating him was to make a thorough overhaul of all the drinking places and dives frequented by men of the strangler's kidney.

The percentage of chances in favour of finding the quarry depended, Blake knew, on just how secure he should feel —on whether he should have the same contempt for the police that a good many American crooks affected, or whether he should really go to earth until he felt it safe to emerge. Should he decide to follow the latter course, then it was going to be a very difficult matter indeed to dig him out. On the other hand, if he should feel moderately secure, then they had a sporting chance. And it was this sporting chance they were betting on.

To begin with, Blake knew it would handicap their chances considerably if they travelled together. If the murderer, or murderers, of Kennedy's agent had known all the details of his arrival in England, due to the success of their attempts at eavesdropping in the hotel at New York, then it was a pretty safe bet that they also knew Bryant Kennedy had placed matters at the London end in Blake's hands, and, that being so, they would be suspicious of all persons, disguised or otherwise, whom they might suspect of being the famous criminologist and his assistant.

For that reason Blake decided they should work separately, and, to this end, he divided into two areas the different London districts which they would cover in their search.

Piccadilly Circus was taken as a starting point, from which Tinker was to work along Regent Street to Oxford Street, down Oxford Street, as far as the end of Shaftesbury Avenue, then back along Shaftesbury Avenue to Piccadilly Circus, after which, in case he had drawn nothing but blanks, Tinker was to begin a systematic combing of the Soho district, which in itself might take several days, owing to the large number of foreign resorts in the quarter.

If that, too, should prove futile, then a fresh council of war would be held, in case Blake had, likewise, had no success. The latter was to begin with Piccadilly, and from there work his way along through the district surrounding Leicester Square, and so on to the Strand, where, among the numerous haunts of Americans there, it was not unlikely that sooner or later the bird they sought would show up. In the meantime, all they could do was to trust that the net thrown out by Scotland Yard would at least make it impossible for the strangler to slip out of the country, although Blake had little doubt that this would be his earliest aim.

Little did either of them dream as they parted at Piccadilly Circus that evening, each to begin the search, how soon the trail was to be picked up.

Tinker did not attempt to adopt any form of disguise. He wore simply a dark grey lounge suit and cap, the latter pulled well down over his eyes. It was unlikely that the man he sought had ever seen him; he had just finished a long stretch at Sing Sing, and had been in

England only a short time. Therefore, Tinker looked just like a hundred other young men with an idle evening before him.

As for his quarry, he had the description furnished to Blake by the taxi-driver, and, in addition to that, he knew he must be on the watch for a man who, in case he should answer roughly to that description, might also reveal, when not on guard, the mechanical motion of the hands which one might acquire with the Chinese habit of rolling two lacquered walnuts.

With that knowledge to go upon, and armed with a small automatic and his usual little leather case of various instruments which was such a necessary part of the equipment of a detective, Tinker started off up Regent Street, while Blake took his way along Piccadilly.

On various occasions in the past Tinker had found it necessary to investigate dives of all sorts and conditions, and not only in London, but in many other parts of the globe, but it is doubtful if he had ever before covered quite so many as he did during the two hours following his parting with Blake.

Off Regent Street there are numerous small streets and yards, in which there is an amazing number of public-houses of various degrees of respectability, but, good, bad and indifferent, they were alike, the same to Tinker. Not a single "prospect" did he miss, although, in most cases, it took him only a few seconds to decide that none of those present at the time could by any possibility be the man he sought.

From Tinker's point of view it was uninteresting work, for apart from the fact that he did not indulge in alcoholic liquors, even his capacity for lemonades and suchlike was limited. However, as it was part of the Baker Street creed that the rough must be taken with the smooth, he stuck to his job until, with a sigh of relief, he at last found himself at Oxford Circus.

The first area, at least, had been pretty thoroughly combed, and as he stood at the circus debating which side of Oxford Street he should begin with, he wondered grimly how Blake's capacity had carried him through so far.

He finally determined to begin with the right-hand side, although he had made up his mind that for the present he would pass by any night clubs as the hour was too early to expect to find many persons in those resorts.

His combing of the various places in and off Oxford Street was simply a repetition of what had gone before, and he was in far from a pleasant frame of mind when he finally stood at Cambridge Circus, forced to confess that, up to then, he had not seen a single person who might be said to answer to the description of the man he was looking for.

Before continuing along Shaftesbury Avenue, Tinker consulted his watch, and found that he had little more than an hour in which to work before the regular places would close. That would scarcely give him time to get back to Piccadilly Circus in order to meet Blake, as they had arranged, unless he hastened, so, swinging round on his heel, he resumed his quest.

He had walked along to the first place visible, and was about to enter, when suddenly he felt a touch on his arm. He turned sharply, then a flicker of recognition showed in his eyes as he saw that he had been accosted by a man, apparently one of the match-selling brigade, but who was, in reality, one of Sexton Blake's best London spies.

"The guv'nor sent out word for the whole gang to get on the job," he whispered from one corner of his mouth. "I've been 'ere for a couple of hours workin' me way back and forth, but no sign of the bird yet, sir."

Tinker nodded.

It was news to him that Blake had sent out word to his widely-organised system of spies that they, too, were to take a hand in the hunt. Tinker decided that Blake must have thought of this after he had left him at Piccadilly Circus. And, as a matter of fact, that is exactly what had occurred.

"I'm just beginning to work Shaftesbury," Tinker whispered back. "If I strike anything I'll pass on the tip to you."

"If I was you, sir, I'd take a peep into that bowling place along a bit farther. A good many Americans go in there, and our bird might risk that, where he wouldn't risk a pub."

"Good idea! I'll try it after I've been in here. Better follow along in case I need you."

With that they parted, and while Tinker entered the public-house, the pseudo match-peddler moved along in the gutter offering his small stock of wares to the passers-by.

Tinker evidently drew a blank in the saloon, for in less than three minutes he reappeared, and, turning to the right, took his way along towards the underground bowling-alley to which the spy had referred. Tinker had never been in the place before, although he had on occasion patronised the better-known one farther along towards Piccadilly Circus, but which is now no longer existent.

As he descended the stairs he was greeted by the sound of falling pins on the hardwood alleys as the heavy wooden balls were bowled along, and, hard on that, came the regular thud of the balls as they struck the padded wall beyond.

Although American bowls is an adaptation of the English game, for some reason or other it has never proved very popular in England in the newer form, although it is a fine, healthy form of amusement, and Tinker, owing to his frequent visits to America, bowled a fairly good ball.

Therefore he ran no risk of appearing a novice as he entered the place and nodded to one of the markers that he would bowl as soon as one of the alleys became free.

When a glance at the score-board showed him that he would probably have to wait some little time, he made for one of the side benches and, climbing into it, lit a cigarette. Half a dozen others were seated on the bench, either watching the play or waiting for a turn at the alleys, but Tinker saw none among them who might be the man he sought. He turned his attention to the players, and, very slowly, he scrutinised each in turn. Three alleys were going at the time, on one of which a foursome was in progress, while on the other two pairs only were playing.

One of the men playing in the foursome was sufficiently of a similar physique to his quarry that Tinker gave him a very close examination from behind the haze of tobacco smoke, which served him as a screen; but, when the man had turned in his direction he saw that he could nor possibly be a day over thirty, while all the evidence went to show that the man known as Shanghai Charlie was at least forty.

Moreover, the man, obviously of the American tourist type, had a pleasant, open countenance, which Tinker found extremely difficult to reconcile with the physiognomy of a strangler, and he came to the conclusion that, whoever the other might be, he was not Shanghai Charlie.

He dismissed the other members of the foursome as outside suspicion, and turned his attention to the next alley, where one of the pairs was playing. And it was then, as one of the players reached for a ball and poised himself for the stroke, that Tinker's teeth came together with a click.

The man he was gazing at was of the same size and build which he was on the watch for. As described by the taxi-driver, the person who had left the cab at the Venetia had worn a moustache, whereas this man was quite clean-shaven. But that circumstance did not matter much to Tinker, who knew from personal experience how easy it was to assume a hirsute disguise.

He was far more intrigued by the type of the man's physiognomy, which, for all the suggestion he gave of being a person of full-blooded habit, had, nevertheless, an odd pallor of countenance, which, however, was so slight that it would never have attracted the attention of the ordinary observer.

But the practiced eye of Tinker noted it almost at the first glance, and he knew where he had seen just such a pallor before. He had seen it stamped on men who had acquired it behind prison walls, and who had not been at large very long. Tinker was as certain of that as if he had seen the man in actual prison garb.

It isn't easy to fool the experienced police or detective eye about that pallor.

But because Tinker had spotted there in that underground bowling alley a man who had, almost undoubtedly, been behind prison bars at no very distant date, and because, in physical appearance, he was similar to the description of the person for whom Blake and Tinker were on the lookout, that by no means meant to say that the man was Shanghai Charlie.

Tinker decided that the man had all the earmarks of the human brute who was quite capable of strangling a fellow human being, for the hard, coarse mouth, the protruding chin, the narrow, cunning little eyes, and the sharply-back-sloping forehead were easy enough to read. It might be Shanghai Charlie, or it might, on the other hand, be another gentleman of the same ilk, of whom Scotland Yard might be glad to hear.

Tinker allowed his gaze to travel over the big man's opponent at the game, then he scrutinised the other pair who were playing on the last alley. But he gave them but cursory attention, for almost, immediately, his eyes came back to the man who was bowling in the centre alley.

And certainly, whoever he might be, he could bowl a strong and well-directed ball, for twice running Tinker saw the whole triangle of pins go down under a single stroke.

It was easy enough for him to study the man at his leisure, for, like the other spectators, he could profess deep interest in the progress of the game. Mindful of what Blake had told him, Tinker did not lose a single motion made by the other.

While actually in action on the alley, he was too intent on the game and occupied by the big wooden balls to reveal himself in any of his usual mannerisms, but it was when he stood aside for his opponent to play that Tinker concentrated most closely on him.

As the score mounted it was plain that the big man felt more and more certain of winning, for where, at the beginning, he had closely watched every one of his opponent's shots, he now relaxed his vigilance a little, and occasionally glanced at one of the alleys on either side. Following that, he made for the third time a "ten strike," and, with the laugh of one who is already tasting the fruits of victory, he lit a cigarette and leant against the end of the runway by which the balls were returned by the boy at the other end of the alley.

Tinker bent forward a little so as not to lose a single movement of the other. He saw him reach down and hand a ball to his opponent, who, after weighing it, rejected it and chose a smaller one. The big man made some remark which the other failed to notice, then, as he replaced the cigarette in his mouth, his right hand dropped idly on to the nearest ball in the runway.

Tinker saw his thick fingers run idly round and round the surface of the polished ball, the while he smoked and watched his opponent. He next took a glance at the score, which caused him to frown. Evidently he was less ahead than he had thought.

Looking along the alley, Tinker could see that only one pin had been left standing, and the big man's opponent was now poising himself for the run in the hope of making his ten on the third ball.

But Tinker paid no attention to that.

His eyes had reverted to the dangling right hand of the big man, and, even as the other made his run and released the ball, Tinker saw the fingers on that dangling right hand close and mechanically work round and round and round against the palm, just as he had seen a Chinaman perform the same action when rolling a couple of lacquered walnuts.

Tinker turned the handle and jerked open the door. Then he jumped back
with a startled glance as a bulky form plunged into the room. Tinker recognised the piggy eyes of the strangler, furious with insane anger. Then they
crashed together in a deadly embrace. *(Chapter 5.)*

THE movement of the fingers continued for perhaps a minute or so, then they came to rest as abruptly as they had begun. The player at the alley had completed his stroke, and had succeeded in taking the last pin. The big man had turned as soon as he had witnessed this, and his little eyes had swept rapidly over the few assembled spectators.

There was a sinister something in that glance that seemed to be asking a question. Had it to do, Tinker was wondering, with that brief, though tell-tale, movement of the fingers?

He could not tell, but now all intention of visiting other resorts along the street had vanished. This man, whom he had found in the underground bowling alley, might or might not be the man he was seeking. Shanghai Charlie might be the criminal for whom he was looking, and this man might be Shanghai Charlie.

Again, he might not, but that one minute, during which the man had displayed the exact mannerisms for which Sexton Blake had told him to be on the watch, was sufficient to cause Tinker to stick to the other like a leech.

He could not tell how long he would have to wait for his quarry to make a move. He did not even know if the man was alone, or if one of the other players was his companion. His immediate concern now was to get out of playing, for, if he took his turn at one of the alleys he would run the risk of having his man give him the slip.

So, when one of the alleys became free, and the marker glanced towards him, Tinker shook his head.

He realised the wisdom of this a few minutes later, when the big man and his opponent finished their match, and apparently decided not to play again. Tinker sat, apparently engrossed in one of the other matches, white the big man donned his coat, and he was still sitting just like that when the other paid the marker and moved towards the staircase.

Tinker noticed that he was leaving alone, so, as soon as the bulky figure had disappeared from view, he yawned and slid from his seat.

He attracted no attention as he made his way past the head of the alleys and towards the stairs. He could see no sign of his quarry as he mounted, but no sooner did he reach the street than he saw his man walking briskly along on the same side. Just close at hand was the pseudo match seller, and, with a meaning look in his direction, Tinker took up the chase.

At that hour in the evening some of the earlier theatres were just disgorging their crowds, and in the crush it was by no means easy to keep his quarry in view, despite his bulk. On the other hand, it was safer under cover of the crowds for him to lessen the distance between them than it would have been an hour earlier or an hour later.

Tinker took the risk, and he was less than ten yards behind when suddenly the quarry turned a corner.

Tinker whipped round after him, and then slowed up as he saw that there were fewer pedestrians here, and that, for some distance at least, he would have little difficulty in keeping his man in sight, since the street led directly into Soho.

He risked an occasional glance behind to see if the "match seller" had followed, and when he was some fifty yards or so along he thought he saw the spy turn into the street, but he could not be quite sure.

He now concentrated all his faculties on the man ahead, but when the other had crossed Old Compton Street, and then turned into a narrow, almost deserted thoroughfare, Tinker was forced to alter his tactics. He knew how quickly a suspicious man would spot a following figure who kept altogether to the pavement. But Tinker was a past master in the art of doorway dodging, and he now brought all his finesse in the art into play.

It was a masterly bit of business the way he slipped from shadowy doorway to shadowy doorway, until he had rounded the next corner and discovered that his quarry had come to a pause before a narrow, dingy-looking, three-storied edifice, which bore all the earmarks of being one of the numerous low-class lodging-houses which are to be found throughout Soho, where such a hodge-podge of the foreign element in London congregates.

Tinker went to cover as silently as a shadow. It would have needed the eye of a night animal to spot that shadow which sank into the dark recess of a doorway. Listening intently, Tinker heard the faint clump of the other's heels on the steps as he mounted. There followed a brief pause, then the sound of a closing door.

"Gone in," he muttered. "There wasn't time for him to ring and for someone to come, which means the door was either unlocked or he had a latch key. In any event, it looks as if that was his hang-out for to-night at least. I'll just see what I can discover."

With that Tinker stole out from the shelter of the doorway and sped swiftly across the street. There he stood behind the trunk of a stunted tree, while he examined the face of the house his quarry had entered. There seemed to be no light on the ground floor, but in the room on the first floor, immediately above the door, a light was burning, and even as Tinker watched the blind he saw a bulky shadow cross it.

"Looks like a pretty good bet that the husky has entered that room," he reflected. "But I think that light was there before he went in. At any rate, there was a light in one of the rooms, and none of the others seem to be lighted now. If that is so, there may have been someone else in the room before he went up. I'd give something to have a peep inside, just to see what the chap is up to. I'll have a try at the door, anyway."

With this Tinker crossed the street again, and after a swift look up and down the street, mounted the steps. He knew pretty well the type of house he had come to, and he was not at all surprised when the door failed to open under his pressure.

It was typical of those one-night lodging-houses which shelter all sorts of queer wrack thrown up by the night tide —a haven where, for money in advance, any night creature can get a bed, and no questions asked. They are the sort of houses which frequently yield a good catch when Scotland Yard makes one of its periodical raids. And Tinker knew just what he should have to avoid once he was inside.

The fact that the door was on a spring lock did not worry him very much, for he had brought his small leather case of instruments, which contained half a dozen supple steel objects that possessed various uses of which the lad was a master, and it did not take him more than a few seconds to select a particularly slender one which he had dubbed the "spider."

With that instrument in his hand, the ordinary lock was as easy to open as if he had possessed the right key, and on this occasion it proved its worth, as usual. In less than ten seconds Tinker had forced the bolt back, and in another five he was inside the lower hall of the house, with the door closed behind him.

As he had guessed from the street, there was no light in the lower hall, but at the back he could see a faint glow, which he knew, must come from the basement, where, he had no doubt, the frowsy owner of the place was esconced in readiness for any business the night might bring.

Tinker did not attempt to extend his investigations in that direction. Instead, he felt cautiously for the handrail of the staircase, and when his fingers had encountered it he lifted his foot and felt for the first step.

He had little fear of anyone whom he might encounter on the staircase, for the type of person who frequented the place would probably be just as anxious to avoid being scrutinised as was Tinker. Among the fraternity there was an unwritten law that no questions should be asked, and Tinker certainly had no intention of breaking it.

He had entered the place for just one purpose, and if he could accomplish that he was quite prepared to give free passage to a dozen night-birds without inquiring their business.

He had no desire to arouse the curiosity of whoever might be in the basement, or although in the event of being discovered he could always bluff that he wanted a room for the night, he wanted to reach his objective unheard and unseen if possible. Therefore, he began to mount the stairs with infinite caution, taking the risk that an occasional creak would not attract much attention in that house.

He succeeded in reaching the top without having roused anyone, so far as he could see, and as he swung round at the top and faced towards the front of the house, he saw a slit of light under a door at the other end of the hall.

He tiptoed along towards this until he came to the foot of the stairs leading to the upper floor, the lower step of which was only a matter of some four feet from the door before which Tinker stood. He felt behind him to locate the rail, in case he should have to use the second staircase for strategic purposes, then he crouched down and applied his eye to the keyhole.

At first he could make out little of the interior of the room owing to some bulky object which cut off most of his view, but it was evident that there was more than one person inside, for he could hear the murmur of voices.

Then, as the bulky object moved, he was able to see clear across the room to a table by the window; and at this table he saw sitting a small, weasel-faced man from whose thin lips a half-smoked cigarette was dangling.

In a flash there came into Tinker's mind Bryant Kennedy's description of Rat the Finn, who had been a running mate of Shanghai Charlie before the latter had gone "up the river," as they say in New

York when a criminal has been sent to Sing Sing.

And if he needed anything further to strengthen his conviction that he had actually picked up the trail of Shanghai Charlie, he had it in the sight of Rat the Finn.

Almost immediately after, Tinker discovered that the bulky object, which had partially obstructed his view, was nothing more nor less than the back of the strangler, who was moving about the room in a nervous manner. It had evidently been he who had been speaking, for now the low rumbling of the voice stopped, and as he watched the Finn, Tinker saw his lips move.

And although the voice was high-pitched and of far less volume than that of the strangler, it was just because of this that every word carried distinctly to the lad who was listening outside the door.

"Aw say, cull, you don't mean it now, do you?" the Rat was whining. "You ain't goin' tu loin me down thataway. Why, Shang, ain't I been the real pal to you all the time you was up the river? What sort of a boid du you think I am? You know dunged well I've stood by you ever since that boid of a stool pigeon double crossed you, bo.

"An' didn't I bump him off as soon as I got the chance? I ain't no gunman, but I got that boid slick for you, Shang. An' now you wants tu go and make a toin like you say. I tell you, Shang, you git in dutch if you do.

"Wait, bo, let me go on. I tell you I don't like this coised town. I want tu get back tu the big boig again. I don't feel right, away from the big town —New York. These boids of gum shoes in this town make me noivous, I'm tellin' you, Shang. A big town cop I can spot and slip, but these boids they call bobbies in this town have got my angora, believe me, Shang.

"I tell you, it ain't safe. If we get pulled on this side, good-night noise and rock us gently. We go fer a long stretch. In the big town, you know, we can fight on our own ground. It's the game we know, Shang.

"Let's go back. What, you want tu go tu Paris fer, anyway? I don't like the sound of that town. I want tu get back to the big burg, Shang. We've sprung the shinies, so what more du you want? If these boids in this town spot that you are on this side, Shang, they'll grab you like a hot dog, believe me.

"You listen tu me, cull. Besides, there's Big Tim waiting for his share of the stones, Shang. If we double cross him he'll make the big town too hot fer us, and it'll mean a spell up the river or the chair fer me over that gumshoe business. Now, you listen tu me, Shang. I'll toke a toin at anyt'ing back in the big town, but this here burg full of these boys they calls bobbies it's gut me, bo —it's gut me."

"Shut yer face, you whining rat! Do you think I'm goin' back tu the big town now with a fat haul like this? What can Big Tim do? If he tries to 'get' me I'll beat him to it, and when I get through with him all he'll need is a coffin. Do you get me?"

"Shang, if you bumped off Big Tim you would have a hundred boids in the big town looking for you, each with a pair uv guns. They'd get you, bo— they'd get you! Shang, I've been a good pal, but I can't make this toin. I can't do it, bo. I want tu get back tu the big town. I don't feel safe here, Shang."

Even Tinker was appalled at the heavy flow of vile recrimination which was loosened at that moment by Shanghai Charlie, he moved across until the bulk of his body again shut off most of Tinker's view, but the strangler had not taken the trouble to lower his tone, with the result that every word reached the lad. It was a nauseating flood which sickened him to listen to, but which, nevertheless, told its own tale.

While a good deal of what Rat the Finn had said would have been cryptic to the average Londoner, Tinker's work had taken him to New York so often that he understood the argot talked on the east side of the "big town," and from the words used and the pronunciation of such words as "noivous" for nervous, "boid" for bird, and "toin" for turn, stamped Rat the Finn as the product of that district as definitely as if he had born a label to that effect.

And, understanding the street argot of the Rat, he had gathered no small amount of information. It had been plain that Rat the Finn was nervous of London, and had some sort of deep fear of the London police. He had been pleading with the strangler to return to New York, but it appeared that the strangler was contemplating making a bolt for Paris with the "shinies," which word didn't need much deduction on Tinker's part to cause him to conclude that the "shinies" were more than likely the missing box of sapphires.

And he had learned more than that from Rat the Finn's whining plea. He had learned that a person known as Big Tim, in New York, had a claim to a portion of the loot, and that Shanghai Charlie was intending to double-cross this person, while the thought of doing so added to the terror of Rat the Finn.

And it seemed, too, that, during the time Shanghai Charlie had been incarcerated in Sing Sing, Rat the Finn had "bumped off," or, in other words, killed, the stool pigeon who had given away the strangler to the police.

Rather a complicated condition of affairs, but quite clear to Tinker, who could follow just what each reference meant. All this he was lining out in his mind while he listened to the appalling curses which Shanghai Charlie was pouring out on to the head of his weaker-kneed, but evidently loyal, fellow-crook.

Then, as abruptly as the strangler had begun, he stopped.

Tinker peered closer, but a movement of the bulky body inside completely shut off his view. The obstruction seemed to be drawing nearer to the door, and, in a sudden panic that some sound might have caught the ear of Shanghai Charlie, Tinker drew back and crouched at the foot of the stairs.

He heard something touch the door on the inside, and with the speed of a squirrel, Tinker was up the second flight of stairs, and lying flat on his stomach round the turn of the handrail above.

Peering down, he again heard the murmur of voices inside the room beneath; then came a silence, broken at irregular intervals of a few seconds by faint sounds, which Tinker could not interpret. They might have been the ordinary sounds made by someone moving about the room. They might have been caused by the shifting of light pieces of furniture.

He could not tell, and presently they stopped. And following that, Tinker saw how wise he had been to retreat when he had first became alarmed, for, without the slightest warning, the door of the room was flung open, and, with remarkable agility for one of his bulk, Shanghai Charlie emerged, and drew the door almost closed after him. He paused then, and, turning towards the opening, spoke as if addressing a final word to the other person in the room.

"All right," he said, in a casual tone, "I'll get some cold ham and a couple of bottles of beer. Are you sure you don't want anything else?"

Then followed the whining intonation, which Tinker had heard when Rat the Finn had been speaking.

"Nothing else for me, Joe —just the ham and the beer will do."

"All right!" And, with that, Shanghai Charlie closed the door and began to descend the stairs, while Tinker wondered why Rat the Finn should have addressed him as "Joe."

He decided it was simply the name by which the strangler was known in the lodging-house, which seemed reasonable enough, seeing he was a fugitive from justice.

Tinker lay where he was until he heard Shanghai Charlie descend the stairs. But as soon as the sound of the front door being closed reached him, he was on his feet like a flash, and went down the stairs two at a time. He had just one thought in his mind, and that was that, while he had the chance, he would make sure of Rat the Finn in any event, and trust to Blake's spy outside to pick up the trail of the strangler.

As he went down he drew out his automatic, and gripped it ready in his right hand. With the strangler out of the way, he did not care now whether other tenants of the place heard him or not. If they bothered him, he knew he could soon put the breeze up them by revealing his identity, so it was with a confident feeling that Rat the Finn would not be a very difficult proposition that he rapped sharply on the door.

No answer.

That did not surprise him much, since the type of person who frequented that class of house was usually a gentleman of retiring disposition. So Tinker rapped a second time.

Still Rat the Finn failed to respond, so without more ado Tinker turned the handle, and entered. He stepped smartly across the threshold, and thrust the door closed behind him; then he stood rigid, staring at the crumpled figure which was doubled up on the floor by the table.

It was plain enough now why Rat the Finn had not answered his summons, or, indeed, would never answer another.

He had gone to his last accounting, and, even as he stood there, Tinker knew that, while he had crouched at the head of the staircase outside, Shanghai Charlie had deliberately strangled his partner — strangled him as ruthlessly as he would a chicken.

Tinker came out of his momentary stupefaction with a jerk. Rat the Finn, who could have told them much, was dead!

He did not need to make any detailed examination to know that. No living man ever lay with his neck twisted in that odd fashion. Then, Rat the Finn must wait for the present, for it had flashed upon

Tinker that, for a second time, Shanghai Charlie had used his strange ventriloquial powers to make his get-away.

He had put those last words Tinker had heard into the mouth of a man who was already dead, just in case some passing tenant should have seen him emerge from the room. That was certain, and it was equally certain that, once he was safely away from the house, he would never come back again.

As Tinker realised this he turned swiftly, and made for the door. He was determined to go after the strangler if he could pick up the trail. It had been a mistake to allow him to get away, he realised now. But once he picked up the trail again he would not drop it until he had got his man cornered.

He turned the handle and jerked open the door.

Then he jumped back with a startled gasp as a bulky form plunged into the room. Tinker recognised the piggy eyes of the strangler, furious with an insane anger.

Then they crashed together in a deadly embrace.

Blake was at the threshold the moment when Shanghai Charlie lifted his foot and drove the sash of the window clean out. There was a crash of glass as the shattered panes tumbled to the ground outside, and then the strangler leaped through the opening without pausing to judge the distance. (*Chapter 6.*)

SCARCELY conscious, however, of his act, Tinker pulled the trigger of his automatic the moment of Shanghai Charlie's rush. But what it did do was to save Tinker from being grasped at the throat in the first onset, for the flash had blinded the strangler for the moment, and in that instant Tinker had eluded the groping fingers.

Tinker's mind was working fast —as fast as minds can only work in moments such as this.

It was all too plain to him now how Shanghai Charlie had fooled him. Even before he left the room he must have been on the qui vive, and his bluff at the door had been but a part of the caution he had displayed.

Apparently he had not remained satisfied that, because the halls were in darkness there could be no one about, and on reaching the lower floor he had opened and shut the street door as a blind, himself remaining inside to watch the door of the room on the upper floor.

He must have heard Tinker descend from the upper floor and open the door of the room. He would know that his crime had been discovered, and at that he had gone up the stairs like a panther.

The sequel was his discovery of Tinker, and, although he could scarcely know the identity of the lad, the expression of his eyes revealed plainly enough his intention that the room should have a second victim.

Tinker did not need the sight of the huddled figure of Rat the Finn, or the memory of the murder in the taxi to enable him to realise that the strangler would most assuredly finish him if he could.

And once he got those powerful fingers into Tinker's throat, the lad would not stand the ghost of a chance.

In the shock of the collision the automatic was knocked from Tinker's hand, and a deft kick on the part of the strangler shot it across the floor and under the table. But if the bullet had not served to stop the crook's rush, the sound of the shot could hardly have escaped notice by some of the other occupants of the house, and, despite the sort of place it was, the proprietor would not dare allow it to pass without inquiry owing to fear of the police.

That was one thing Tinker was counting on, and the reason why, even in the first heat of the struggle, he was fighting for time as his chief ally. But if Tinker was figuring along those lines, so was Shanghai Charlie, and, despite the eel-like twistings of the sturdy lad, he carried him back against the wall by the sheer weight of his bulk.

Tinker made a feint, and followed up by trying to slip through the other's grasp to the floor, from which position he hoped he might be able to upset the strangler; but a wicked up-thrust of the latter's knee sent the lad sagging in a terrible agony of pain, and the next moment the thug had him by the throat.

Tinker's eyes almost burst with sudden blindness as his antagonist bore in with a fury that was almost unbelievable. No human being could have withstood that terrible and expert pressure. It cut off the mental and nervous control of Tinker's being for the time as completely as if he had been divided into two insensate physical units. He was a limp bit of sagging bone and flesh, dangling like a stuffed sawdust doll in that crushing grip —nothing else. And he would have been hurled to the floor as dead as a wrung chicken had not the door opened at that moment.

It was the frowsy owner of the dive, a villainous looking creature, who, though he didn't care two straws if his tenants killed each other out of hand, knew how short his shrift would be if the police came on the scene. It would not be an easy matter to explain that crumpled rag of humanity on the floor, let alone the second outrage he was now witnessing.

And in order to back up his intervention he was carrying a heavy revolver in his right hand, while a long-bladed knife gleamed in the other.

Of this Tinker saw nothing.

His eyeballs had been turned up beneath the lids by the awful pressure in the arteries which served the brain. But Shanghai Charlie jerked to one side like lightning as he caught sight of the blue barrel of the revolver, he did not pause to parley. Instead, he withdrew one hand from Tinker's throat and grasped the lad about the waist. Then he lifted him bodily and hurled him full at the utterly dumbfounded man who had just entered.

Tinker struck him midway between chest and knees, and as both went down the strangler kicked the table half across the room. It came to rest on one side between him and the tangled heap which represented Tinker and the cursing owner of the place. Then the crook, with an agility extraordinary in one of his bulk, cleared both table and humans at a single leap and went down the stairs like a suddenly released avalanche.

What reveals more than anything else about the exact type of place Tinker had entered is the fact that, with the exception of the owner, not another tenant even opened the door of his room to investigate the cause of the disturbance. No one attempted to arrest the flight of the strangler as he tore open the street door and dashed out.

But even before he reached the bottom of the steps two figures loomed up before him, and ere he could stop himself, Shanghai Charlie had bowled one of the pair over, while the next instant he found himself rolling in the gutter in the grip of a man he sensed instinctively was as powerful as himself, and who, moreover, had a deadly counter to every strangling trick he possessed.

That man was Sexton Blake.

And in order to understand just how that pair arrived on the scene at such a critical moment it is necessary to take some cognisance of Sexton Blake's movements after he had parted from Tinker in Piccadilly Circus.

It will be recalled that just as he had swung into Shaftesbury Avenue Tinker had encountered one of the numerous army of spies — or, rather, agents —whom Blake employed on occasion. The organisation of this system had not been a matter of weeks or months, but of years, and its personnel included men and women in all walks in life.

Its ramifications, as a matter of fact not only embraced London and its suburbs, but stretched throughout the British Isles, and it is extremely doubtful if any other foe of the evildoer, except Blake, could have built up such an organisation.

Its strings stretched all the way from prominent bankers, lawyers, solicitors, professors, and other professional and business men, down to some of the toughest old lags to be found out of prison. And it is a tribute to the confidence in which Blake was held by certain members of the latter class that on more than one occasion they had rendered him signal assistance against the members of the fraternity to which they belonged, or had belonged.

Thus it was that in pondering matters over as he walked up Piccadilly after leaving Tinker, Blake made a sudden decision to bring his own private spy machinery into action. In figuring matters out, Blake came to the conclusion that the chances of Shanghai Charlie being still in hiding in London were stronger than the chances that he had managed to make a get-away. A dispassionate analysis of the several items of information which he had so far managed to collect seemed to point that way.

If this should be so, then he realised that if the search —apart from that being conducted by the Yard —was confined to the efforts of himself and Tinker, the strangler might elude them for days, since it was out of the question for them to devote all their time to the affair. But with certain elements of his private spy organisation brought into play, it would mean that some of the shrewdest heads in every quarter of the great city would be pitted against the strangler, and, since it was very unlikely that the New York crook would have any intimate friends London, Blake didn't think there was much risk of his being double-crossed.

So it was with that decision that he turned into the Venetia as he passed, and sent through a phone call to a certain number in the East End, which would, he knew, bring into play the particular squad he desired with extra ordinary rapidity.

Then Blake had continued his way up Piccadilly to begin a survey of the area which he had allotted to himself.

It had been a comparatively simple matter at the beginning, for there were few places along the famous thoroughfare where gentlemen of the strangler's kidney were likely to be found. But Blake was missing no chances, and for that reason his investigation was as careful as if he had been searching a very different quarter.

It was when Blake had almost worked his way back to Piccadilly Circus that he was approached by a seedy-looking individual, who mumbled a few words out of the corner of his mouth. Blake gave a barely perceptible nod; but the next moment he had altered his course, and was crossing the Circus at a quick stride towards Shaftesbury Avenue.

Those few words had been the message passed along by means of several of his spies from the pseudo match-seller who had first communicated with Tinker and had then followed the lad's trail when he had left the bowling-alley. As he passed along the Avenue a very close observer might have noticed that from time to time other seedy-looking persons brushed close to Blake, but they would scarcely have guessed that on each occasion Blake received a further message.

By the time he had reached the street by which Shanghai Charlie and Tinker had entered Soho, Blake was in possession of all that had occurred; and as he turned into the foreign quarter he received a signal from the pseudo match-seller. Blake signed for the other to approach, and a few seconds later he knew that Tinker had followed his quarry into a house farther on.

"Come along!" was all he said.

With that he lengthened his stride, and he and his companion had just reached the steps of the dive into which the latter had seen Tinker disappear, when the door was flung open, and a burly figure dashed out.

It is known that it was the strangler in flight, but before either Blake or his companion could interfere the latter was bowled over and sent crashing against the stone pavement with a force that nearly cracked his skull, and which had the effect of rendering him hors do combat.

That momentary check was sufficient for Blake to recover himself. Before the strangler could plunge past him Blake had grappled, and the pair went rolling into the gutter as each fought for a controlling grip.

If the strangler soon discovered he was now at grips with a very different type from his usual victims, Blake on his part, was equally quick to grasp that, whether his antagonist was Shanghai Charlie or not, he was at least a professional strangler; for at the first instant of contact Shanghai Charlie had endeavoured to work his hands up into Blake's throat in a way that the detective had encountered more than once in the past.

There is something about the methods of the strangler, the dacoit, the thug, and the knifeman which distinguishes those who use one of those methods from all other types of criminals. And in the strangler there is, in addition, a something terrible, a cold and deadly purpose that makes itself felt at the first moment of contact as repulsively ruthless as the dart of a cobra.

If was that "something" which Blake felt, and which at once brought into play every counter he had ever acquired during his long career, when on so many occasions his own wit and his own strength had been all that stood between him and violent death.

Shanghai Charlie knew only too well that, if he were to stand any chance at all of making a get-away he must break free before assistance reached his antagonist. He did not know that the second man was lying unconscious on the pavement, but he realised that the owner of the dive would be almost certain to raise a hue and cry in order to keep himself right with the police; while he had seen sufficient of the lad, whom he had so nearly succeeded in strangling, to know that once he recovered himself enough to pick up his pistol he would be on the warpath again. Therefore he redoubled his efforts to get his powerful fingers planted in his antagonist's throat, for he knew once he achieved that he would soon make short work of Blake.

But never before had the strangler found himself countered so effectually, and not only countered, but a sharp and strange offensive brought into play as well.

For Sexton Blake's mind was figuring just about one jump ahead of Shanghai Charlie's. Blake knew he had to hold his man, even if he couldn't overpower him, until assistance should arrive. But as Blake began to feel the faint yielding on the part of the other, when a thrill of exultation passed through him as he slowly but surely worked his way on top of the strangler, Shanghai Charlie, who was in a sudden panic which he had never felt in his life before, made one supreme effort and broke free. Before Blake could recover his advantage the strangler had rolled to one side, bringing up against the kerb with a thud. Then he was on his feet, and while Blake was still grasping the thin air, had bolted straight up the steps and back into the dive.

The detective was after him like a flash. There was sheer panic in that sudden bolt of the crook's, and Blake know only too well what utterly mad deeds a man is capable of when in that state. He couldn't figure out why the strangler had chosen to re-enter the dive instead of taking his chances by a dash down the street, but Blake was determined to overtake him and settle the affair once and for all.

Blake took the steps two at a time, barely conscious that his spy was lying unconscious on the pavement. Nor did he know that the figure he hurled aside as he flew down the hall was none other than his own assistant Tinker, who, as he shot the light of his electric torch after the fleeing figure, was amazed to recognise Blake. Tinker was off in pursuit, but by the time he had started Blake was already through the door at the end of the hall, where a strange scene met his eyes.

That the strangler had gone that way was evident, for two very suspicious-looking individuals, who had been seated at a table in the room, were now crouching in one corner, while the table had been hurled aside, and the strangler himself was at the window, one hand holding a pistol with which he menaced the pair.

Blake was at the threshold at the moment when Shanghai Charlie lifted his foot and drove the sash of the window clean out. There was a crash of glass as the shattered panes tumbled to the ground outside, and without pausing to judge the distance, the strangler leaped through the opening.

Blake covered the distance in a couple of leaps, and flashed through with as little regard for what lay beneath as the other had shown. As a matter of fact, there was a good six foot drop, but Blake had landed with bent knees, and beyond a rough shock he escaped unscathed. He stumbled to his feet just as the strangler turned and pulled the trigger.

There was a spitting flash of flame, but the bullet sped harmlessly past Blake. Shanghai Charlie was more expert with his hands than with a gun.

Blake heard the strangler go threshing about in the dark, then there came another crash of glass. He could scarcely see his surroundings, but knew enough about the probable arrangement of the place to guess that the crook had broken the window of another house which backed on the small yard at the rear of the dive.

He took the time to drag out his pocket torch, and as he pressed the switch he saw that he was right, for the bulk of the strangler was just disappearing through the broken sash. Blake jerked to one side as the strangler again lifted his arm, then he hurled himself forward, dragging out his own gun as he went.

To his surprise, the fugitive did not shoot again, nor did he attempt to prevent Blake from climbing through the back window of the dive. Blake switched on the torch again, and found that he was in a sort of kitchen which was quite unfurnished, with the exception of a rusty stove.

A door opposite him was open, and he made for it.

Up above somewhere he could hear the clatter of the strangler's boots as he raced along an uncarpeted hall. It was that sound that told Blake they had entered an uninhabited house.

He marked the bottom of the stairs, then he switched off the torch and started up. He reached the top in safety, but as he swung round into what he knew was the hall there came another slitting flame ahead, and a bullet thudded into the wall uncomfortably close to his head.

Blake shot twice then flung himself aside and took two flying leaps along the hall.

The strangler began shooting wildly, until suddenly Blake heard the hammer come down with a harmless click, telling him that the other had used his last chamber.

Blake shot low twice more; then as he started on again he felt himself driven back by a perfect whirlwind of fury. The strangler was filled with both rage and panic —a dangerous combination as Blake realised —and once more he went down, bringing into play all his wits and cunning to counter those terrible hands which were searching for his throat.

Blake yielded for the fraction of a second while the strangler, quick as a snake to seize his chance, made just the move Blake had lured him to. Then there came a hoarse cry as Blake gave a sudden twist, and the next instant, as Tinker reached the top of the stairs, his electric torch playing on the bare floor ahead of him, a strange sight was brought to his eyes.

He saw Blake squirming over on top of the strangler, the while he forced the latter's right arm up and up and up between his shoulders. The strangler was using every atom of his great strength to break that hold which was giving him excruciating pain, but inch by inch Blake forced the face downwards to the floor. Tinker ran forward, reversing his automatic as he went.

"Let me get him with this, guv'nor," he cried.

"Keep away!" panted Blake. "Leave me to settle this thug."

And Tinker, knowing only too well when to obey, stood by, holding the light trained on the pair while Blake's left hand worked up beneath the strangler's chin until his fingers curled in slowly but remorselessly.

It was the strangler's own hold used on himself, and as Tinker saw, his mouth set in grim admiration while he watched Sexton Blake throttle and throttle that wagging head until it sank lower and lower, and finally, accompanied by a sudden convulsion of the great hulking form, fell to the floor.

The stranger had been conquered by his own method —not throttled to death, but rendered as helpless as a trussed chicken.

WITH Shanghai Charlie unconscious, it was not a very difficult matter for Blake's practised fingers to make a swift search of his person, while Tinker held the light, and a sharp exclamation of satisfaction sounded from Blake's lips as, from beneath the strangler's shirt, he took out a heavy packet wrapped in soft flannel.

It took Blake just about ten seconds to satisfy himself that the packet was literally stuffed with scores of uncut stones, which gleamed deeply bluish white under the light —stones that, he felt convinced, could only be the missing Westmore sapphires.

He had just time to drop the packet in the side-pocket of his coat when there came the sound of heavy footsteps in the basement, and as both he and the lad turned their heads they saw the blue helmet of a constable appear.

He strode forward with a gruff: "Now, then, what's all this about?" But Blake, who recognised him, called out:

"It is all right, Smiles. This is Sexton Blake and Tinker. I've landed a bird that I fancy, will be welcomed at the Yard. I guess you had better take him in charge. How did you get here?"

"Oh, is that you, Mr. Blake? I heard a rumpus, and was trying to find out what was going on. I met Dago Joe, who runs a house round the corner, and he said there had been some shooting going on at his place. I came through the back way. What is it, sir? And who have you got here?"

"Have you had any orders to be on the look-out for an American crook known as Shanghai Charlie, who is suspected of murdering the man who was found strangled in a taxi in front of the Venetia?"

"Yes. sir. You don't mean to say you've got him?"

"I have some reason to believe that this man will eventually be identified as the man who is wanted, Smiles. I shall turn him over to you, and you needn't bring my name in —officially —unless it is absolutely necessary."

"That is very good of you, sir. This will be a capture worth while."

"Well, I can tell you where you will find his running mate, who is known as Rat the Finn." put in Tinker, and even Blake glanced at the lad in surprise. "But you won't ever bring him to trial," he went on. "You will find him in the first floor front in Dago Joe's place —dead —strangled by his mate who lies here."

Then, in a few brief words, he related what had happened to him in the dive; although, since Blake had made no mention to the constable about the stones, Tinker avoided any reference to that phase of the conversation which he had overheard between Rat the Finn and Shanghai Charlie.

Needless to say, the constable was only too grateful to have the credit for the capture turned over to him, so there was little difficulty in Blake and Tinker getting away, although, of course, they would both make official statements as to the part each had played in the drama that night.

Once back in Baker Street, Blake made a more detailed examination of the sapphires, becoming more convinced than ever that he had recovered the Westmore gems. But, since he could not get positive identification until Bryant Kennedy should arrive, he dropped them in the safe until Kennedy should put in an appearance. And as far as he and Tinker were concerned, the case might have been called finished, until, a few days later, Bryant Kennedy walked into the consulting room at Baker Street.

When the greetings were over, Blake opened the safe and laid the packet of sapphires before him.

"I suppose you have received sufficient description and inventory from your client to identify them?" he remarked.

"Yes; but I'd like to hear first how you got them," responded Kennedy.

"Check them up first." drawled Blake. "Then I'll tell you the whole yarn."

Kennedy took out some papers which Mrs. Westmore had given him, and set to work. For a quarter of an hour he worked away, comparing each stone with the inventory which he had before him. At the end of that time he looked up.

"No doubt about it, Blake. You have bagged the whole lot. Now, do tell me what happened."

So, lighting a cigar, Blake leant back; and gave the required details. Kennedy listened in silence, glancing now and then from Tinker to Blake; then, as Blake finished, he said in very earnest tones:

"I can't tell you quite what this means to me, Blake. I owe you a very heavy debt of gratitude for what you have done. I shall not try to say more just now, because I know you would rather I wouldn't. But, more than to me, it means so much to the Westmores.

"As I think I told you, I persuaded them to go to my mother's house in Washington Square; but Mrs. Westmore would only consent to do so when I assured her that we should most certainly recover the sapphires. She is a very proud woman, and would not accept anything that smacked of charity.

"By the same assurance, I persuaded her to let me bring a lung specialist to see her, and I am very glad to say that he assures me he can cure her by this new inoculation for tuberculosis which has just been discovered. In addition to that, Thompson, the great spinal specialist, has seen the boy, who has been crippled from some spinal trouble for years, and he believes he can put him right, although it will take a considerable time to do so. Without the proceeds of these stones, Mrs. Westmore would never consent to the treatment, so perhaps you can grasp just how much I —we owe to you in this."

Blake was a trifle surprised at the warmth with which Kennedy spoke. To Blake the case had been all in the ordinary course of things, and, thanks to Tinker having picked up the strangler's trail so soon, it had been brought to a finish much quicker than usual.

In fact, it was a case which Blake looked upon as the simple running to earth of an American crook. But he made no comment. He simply waved Kennedy's thanks aside, and casually suggested that all three should go on to the Venetia for lunch, as Kennedy had announced that he was returning to New York by a steamer which was due to sail from Southampton the following day.

  • • • • •

Some two weeks later, when the American mail was delivered at Baker Street, Blake and Tinker began to understand the inspiration of Kennedy's anxiety to recover the sapphires and his extraordinary gratitude to Blake; for in the post was a letter from him which, after a swift perusal, Blake began to read aloud to Tinker.

"He says this, my lad: 'I am writing you to renew the very deep gratitude which my wife and I—'"

"What!" yelled Tinker. "Wife! What on earth is he talking about, guv'nor? Mr. Kennedy isn't married."

"You wait, Tinker," responded Blake. "You will soon find out whether he is or not." Then Blake proceeded: "'Which my wife and I feel. In London it was not possible for me to take you completely into my confidence, but 1 can now tell you that before leaving New York I had asked Miss Westmore to do me the honour to become my wife.

" 'From what I told you there, you will understand when I say that, for the same reasons which her mother had for refusing my assistance, Miss Westmore refused me. Under the circumstances, it was difficult for me to persist, but on my return from London with the property which you recovered, and which again placed them in a position of independence, she made me the happiest man in the world.

" 'So, as there was no reason for delay, we went to the little church around the corner, and by the time you receive this we shall have left for our honeymoon. Under separate cover I am sending you and Tinker a photograph of my wife, on each of which she has written an expression of her gratitude, but she bids me say that she hopes to be able to have this pleasure personally at an early date.'

"That is all about that, my lad," remarked Brake, with a smile, as he laid the letter down. "This packet here looks as if it might contain photographs. Open it and see."

Tinker obeyed, and a few seconds later took out two large cabinet photographs of Kennedy's wife. She smiled upon them frankly in all the fresh beauty of her newfound happiness, and although Blake was still dumbfounded at the news of Kennedy's marriage —for he had considered him as confirmed a bachelor as himself —he could not but think that the girl upon whom he gazed would make his old friend happy.

And the joint telegram of congratulation which they set to work to compose a few minutes later was a sincere message to both Kennedy and the girl who, as Miriam Westmore, had fought such a brave fight for the mother and the crippled brother who had been left in her care.

When the message was completed, Tinker glanced at Blake.

"I suppose this means a wedding present, guv'nor? What will you send?"

Blake rubbed his chin thoughtfully.

"I don't quite know, my lad. As we are going on to hear sentence pronounced on Shanghai Charlie, we might take the opportunity to stop on the way back and choose something."

And it was an appropriate errand which took them to a certain famous jeweller's that day after hearing the just sentence of death pronounced on the strangler, to choose a gift for the girl whose life the murderous beast had so nearly turned into a long and sad pilgrimage of misery.

At least, that is the way Tinker looked at it.

THE END.
[22100 WORDS]